THE FINAL CHARGE

BY CHARLES GODFREY

THE FINAL CHARGE

Copyright © 2011, by Charles Godfrey.
Cover Copyright © 2011 Sunbury Press. Front cover image "Ghosts of Gettysburg" by Lawrence von Knorr.

NOTE: This is a work of fiction. Names, characters, places and incidents are the product of the author's imagination or are used fictitiously, and any resemblance to actual persons, living or dead, business establishments, events or locales is entirely coincidental.

All rights reserved, including the right to reproduce this book, or portions thereof, in any form or by any means, electronic or mechanical, including photocopying, recording, or by any information storage and retrieval system, without permission in writing from the publisher.

FIRST SUNBURY PRESS EDITION
Printed in the United States of America
May 2011

ISBN 978-1-934597-41-5

Published by:
Sunbury Press
Camp Hill, PA
www.sunburypress.com

Camp Hill, Pennsylvania   USA

Acknowledgments

To my wife, Nancy, and son, Stewart, for their love, support, patience, and understanding during this project, thank you very much.
I would like to thank the following people for their assistance with this project, without their help this book would not have been written.
Raymond Ray, my dear friend who gave me the inspiration to write a book in the first place.
Jeff Jeffery, my first reader, his feedback was critical to the start of this project.
Dave Donnelly, my historian friend. I want to thank you for your input.
Robert Broomall, historian, author, friend, who believed in me along with his Group that he organized.
Sharon Broomall, Chris Vaughn, Dave Hewitt, and Bob Knapp.
In addition, I would like to thank the re-enacting community for their many interactions around the campfires. The comments and dreams all contributed to the realism of this book. The many suggestions that came from organizations such as;
First Maryland Volunteer Infantry Regiment.
Third Maryland Volunteer Infantry Regiment.
Seventh Pennsylvania Volunteer Infantry Regiment.
The National Regiment.
ELF Company in particular. Members such as Bill Wilson, Dale Brennan, Jake Martz, and Christopher Frazier, all helped complete this project.
Thank you all very much.

"It's an adventurous journey through time with the horrors and sorrows of war…"

Prologue

Gettysburg, Pennsylvania
Friday, July 3, 1863 - Midnight

Rain poured over the war-torn fields. Lightning shot across the darkness like cannon fire. From the area known as the Valley of Death, two Confederate cavalrymen ran frantically up the washed-out road as the storm raged around them.

Their heavy footsteps plunged through the thick mud, echoing the pounding of their hearts. Lightning flashed on the soldiers' rough and ghostly faces, revealing one with wide, wild eyes and the other whose eyes were filled with fear. It had been a very long day and the night was no better.

Another bolt of lightning made them quicken their pace. The larger of the two suddenly caught his boot and was thrown to the ground. He landed on the ground with a grunt, the air pushed from his lungs.

He tried to pick himself up, but a hard, sharp pain shot through his side. His body went numb as he fell back down. He rubbed the side of his chest and took short painful breaths. "I think that bastard broke my rib," he said.

"Damn, Earl, hurry up," the wild-eyed man said as he ran back to help his comrade.

"Christ sakes! Get up, we gotta go! There's Union men everywhere."

"My boot is stuck, Jake, and I think my rib is broke."

"Shit," Jake said as he nervously felt along the boot. "It's a God damn tree root," Jake said feeling his way through the mud. He pulled up on the root as hard as he could in an attempt to free his comrade.

With another flash of lightning, Earl pulled his boot, now drenched in dripping muck, out from under the root.

Jake yanked him to his feet. With a gasp, Earl stood upright. They ran until they finally reached their destination: a large red barn. With the rain in their bloody and bruised faces, they felt their way to a small side door.

Jake grabbed the latch and pulled up on it, trying to force the door open. When that failed, he motioned to big Earl to open the door. Earl, realizing the danger of being seen, swallowed his pain and threw his shoulder into the door, breaking it open with a loud crack. Earl gritted his teeth. Quickly, the two men entered the blackness of the barn, shutting the door behind them.

Once inside, they threw off their soaked black slouch hats and tunics and wiped the rain and blood from their foreheads, gasping to catch their breaths.

Earl gingerly felt his ribs, checking the damage. Jake fingered for his matches that were protected by the inside pocket of his jacket. Finding one, he lit it. The vast shadows inside the barn swallowed up the tiny light, but there was just enough to unmask a bench and small wooden table.

Striking a second Lucifer match, Jake lit a lantern sitting on the bench. Its light revealed a hard young face with cuts and bruises. Still rattled, Earl tried lighting another lantern hanging on a post by the table, but his matches were wet and useless.

"Jake, your matches," he demanded, shaking off the chill.

Jake slid the matches across the table. A moment later, the room was lit with an eerie radiance, forming shadows on the walls. The warm light of the lamp revealed Earl's beaten face.

Jake quickly turned his attention to the hayloft which ran the length of the back wall. "She said the tinderbox is still there. How did we miss it?

"Deeper under the straw, she said," Earl noted.

"Muh haversack betta be there," Jake warned.

With a lantern in his right hand, Jake started for the hayloft with Earl following right behind him. Jake got to the wooden ladder and started to climb. Earl stumbled trying to keep up.

"Come on, be careful!" Jake said, waving the lantern towards Earl's face.

When they got to the top, they crawled to the far corner where Earl had put the black haversack under one of the floor boards. Clearing the straw, Earl said, "Should be 'bout right here."

He felt around the floor and found the loose board he was looking for. His chest stung as he pried it up and leaned it against a beam. Under the board was a hollowed-out joist. In the space provided was the black haversack. A slight smile came across Earl's face. He reached down and grabbed it. Jake motioned for the sack.

"Here," Earl said.

"Is the tinderbox there?" Jake asked.

After removing even more straw from the joist, Earl peered into the hollow, "Yes." He reached down and brought out the box. "Straw was over it. That's how I missed it."

"Over here," Jake said.

Earl handed Jake the box. It was a tin box with a pentagram scratched into the lid. Jake began to open the box slowly. Inside were an hour glass and a piece of parchment with the words, *Tempus Fugit* written.

He carefully removed the hourglass and placed it on the floor. The white crystal sands began to pour. Nervously he picked up the parchment and unrolled it, revealing a poem. Jake handed the parchment to Earl. "From the look of the glass timer, you got 'bout three minutes to read this," Jake said.

Earl stared at the words written on the slip of paper and then handed it back to Jake.

"Don't ya' wanna read it? She's your friend. Don't you wanna go to that world you talked 'bout? Or does the hangman's noose sound better to ya?" Jake asked.

"Dunno how to read." Earl simply said.

Jake was speechless, he peered at the timer and saw that the powdery white crystals were halfway done funneling through and were producing little sparkles as they fell.

"Barely read myself," Jake said and began to read the poem.

> "Many paths through centuries fall-
> If change is what you seek.
> Illumination shines true for all-
> Fulfillment for the meek."

As he finished reading, they waited for the last grain of sand to drop from the glass. The two deserters looked at each other in disappointment. An eerie silence came over the barn. The rain that had been pattering on the roof had stopped.

"We still here and you haven't changed one bit, you ugly bastard." Jake grumbled.

"Don't think it worked?" Earl asked.

"No, you fool!"

"Look, let's put everything back and check outside to see if anything changed," Earl suggested, "We can hide here if'in it ain't."

Earl put the hourglass and the parchment back in the tinderbox. When he started to put the haversack back, Jake stopped him.

"Shit, we've been through that, and I'm not 'bout to repeat. Gimmy me that bag."

But Earl held on tightly to the haversack.

Jake grabbed the sack: Earl tightened his grip. Jake stared, then let go. Earl looked back at Jake with an empty victory smile. Jake returned the smile as he covertly reached into his boot, pulling out a large bowie knife.

He lunged forward and thrust the knife into Earl's chest, twisting it as he pulled it back out. Earl's smile was replaced by a look of horror.

Jake stared at Earl. "There's just not enough for the two of us."

Jake put his knife back into his boot as he looked around. As the adrenaline faded from his veins, Jake grabbed the haversack and lantern and then shimmied over to the ladder. He looked down into the dark barn and even with the lantern, he couldn't see anything clearly. He climbed onto the ladder, and then looked back at Earl sitting in the corner staring into nothingness.

The Final Charge

"Don't go anywhere, I'll go check outside fer ya," Jake said sarcastically. He smiled.

He started down the ladder with the lantern in one hand and the haversack over his arm. Suddenly, the rung of the ladder broke and Jake fell to the floor with a thud.

"God damn it," he said lying there. He got up and dusted himself off. He picked up the lantern that was still lit and held it up. "Now, where's muh haversack?"

For a moment, he thought he had lost it. Anger swelled up, but then, there it was. He picked it up and walked toward where the table had been, but the table was nowhere to be found.

Jake looked around the empty floor for his hat and coat. "Where's muh stuff?" He wondered out loud. He started to walk back and have a look, then thought better of it. "No matter now." He started for the side door. He heard a noise and paused at the door to listen. "Who's here?" He asked nervously as he looked around. The air was still. He grabbed the door handle, slowly opened the door, and slid outside.

The rain had stopped and the ground was dry. Jake could see the stars in the early morning sky as he walked onto the road's hard surface. He looked down and wondered: *It was just raining, so why is the road so hard?* After all, it had been pouring rain just a few minutes ago. He stomped his foot on the hard road then looked up to see two balls of fire coming right at him.

A car traveling at fifty miles per hour hit Jake. The black haversack went flying through the air. The car screeched to a stop and a young woman, dressed as a nurse, got out and ran back to him.

There in the street, she saw what appeared to be a reenactor. She looked at her watch. It was close to five. "What in the world was he doing out here this early in the morning?" she whispered to herself. Then she used her cell phone to call 911.

Chapter One

Present Day - 4:30 A.M.

It was July 4th weekend, 2013, Friday morning. A yellow and brown 1974 Ford Bronco emerged from the darkness, carrying a driver and three passengers as it cruised down the road.

Mike Hill, with a calmness in his steel-blue eyes, was behind the wheel. The muscles in his arms filled out his t-shirt. It had been two hours since the last rest stop out of Cumberland, Maryland. With the truck's old air conditioning unit barely keeping the passenger area cool, Mike drove with his left hand gripping the steering wheel and his right resting on his blue jeans. As he gazed out the windshield, he yawned and stretched his muscles to rid the stiffness of the long ride from his six-foot frame.

Mike's best friend, Ray Hensley, rode shotgun. He wore his favorite Confederate flag t-shirt; it complimented his reddish-brown hair. Ray's face was pressed against the window. He shifted every so often in his sleep, leaving steamy breath streaks on the glass. Occasionally, Mike pushed the arm of his slightly overweight friend to wake him. Ray's eyes lazily slit open, then he resumed his slumber.

In the back seat was Gordon Smart, reading by the light of a medical flashlight. Periodically, he would put down his book, *They Met at Gettysburg*, and wipe his vintage, wire-framed glasses with his shirt. He lounged his six-foot, slender frame across the backseat.

Mike, 26, was a medic in the army before joining the Fire Department. Ray worked as an emergency medical technician on the ambulance at the same station as Mike. They grew up together in the same neighborhood. Ray, being two years younger, was always under Mike's wing.

They met Gordon in the Fire Academy. Later, Ray was promoted to paramedic and was assigned at another station across town.

As the Bronco rounded the next hill, its lights illuminated a sign that read: Borough of Gettysburg. Mike stretched his right arm and rubbed the back of his neck. "Wake up you two, we're almost there."

Ray wiped sleep from his eyes and yawned audibly as he slurred, "Great." Then he turned his head back toward the drool marks on the passenger side window, closed his eyes once more, and drifted into a restful slumber.

Gordon patted the side of the driver's seat with his hand in a reassuring manner. "I'm still with you, Mike."

"How's the book?" asked Mike.

"Very interesting, the ordeal they had to endure," Gordon said.

"I feel so bad for 'em," Ray mocked, hearing with his eyes closed.

Mike nudged Ray to get up, but he continued to act as though he was asleep. Mike knew and playfully irritated him. "Get up you lazy bastard!" He smiled in the rear view mirror and glanced at Gordon for approval.

"This being our first outing of the year, Ray, I thought you would be more enthusiastic, but, oh, no, all you want to do is sleep," Mike said.

"That's not true!" Ray said.

"When's the last time you drove?" Mike asked.

"That's beside the point; you like to drive." Ray turned toward the window.

As Mike watched Ray trying to sleep again, he reached toward the center dash, turned on the radio, and cranked up the volume. Ray shot up with a dazed look on his face.

"Sweet home Alabama!" Mike sang along with the radio. His head bobbed to the music as he tapped his hands on the steering wheel. A smile formed on his face as he glanced at Ray waking up. Gordon smiled and leaned over the seat and joined in the singing. "Where the skies are so blue!"

"Turn it down!" Ray cried.

"You awake now?" Mike asked.

"Yes, yes! Just turn it down!"

Mike was about to look at the dash to turn down the radio, when something caught his eye. His headlights exposed a young woman in white standing in the middle of the road.

"Holy shit!" Mike yelled and slammed on the brakes.

Gordon braced himself while Ray stiffened, putting pressure on his imaginary right-side brake. "What the hell!" Ray yelled.

The Bronco skidded sideways, missing the woman by a few feet, as the truck jarred to a halt. Mike turned off the radio.

"What was she doing in the middle of the road?" Mike asked, visibly shaken.

"Who?" Ray asked.

"That girl. Didn't you see her?"

"I didn't see a thing," Ray said.

"How 'bout you Gordy?" Mike asked.

"Sorry Mike."

There was silence as Mike regained his composure.

"She was wearing a long white dress," Mike said.

"So where did she go?" Ray asked.

"Christ, maybe you hit her and she's under the truck," Gordon said anxiously as he got out. Mike followed.

Ray grabbed a flashlight from the glove box and got out to help. Gordon, with his medical light, looked under the truck along with Mike. Ray walked to a nearby ditch and looked in. They all looked around, but she was nowhere to be found.

"Maybe it was your mind playing tricks on you, long drive, lack of sleep. It's four-thirty in the morning," Ray said looking at his watch. They all got back in the vehicle.

"I'm wondering that, too, now," Mike said as he got back behind the wheel.

Gordon shrank back in his seat and took in a deep breath, adjusting his glasses. "Have we calmed down? What did she look like?"

"Yeah, she looked like a civilian reenactor," Mike said still thinking about the girl. He put the Bronco in gear and started to pull out. Just then a car sped by them, almost hitting Mike's door.

"Jesus, that was close," Mike said as he brought the truck to another halt.

"Can you just get us there ... *alive*, is preferable," Gordon said.

A few miles down the road Mike's headlights lit up a standing vehicle with its four-way flashers on, parked in the middle of the road. The driver's door was wide open. As Mike approached the car, he noticed a young woman kneeling over a man lying in the road.

"Freakin' accident!" Mike yelled.

"Same girl?" Ray asked.

"No," Mike said.

All three bailed from the Bronco. Mike got to the injured man first and knelt down beside the girl. He bent over the man and grabbed his shoulders and squeezed them checking his responsiveness. "Are you okay?"

"I think he's dead," the girl said.

The man was on his back. His face was blackened by what appeared to be gunpowder, and he wore a filthy, tattered Confederate Army uniform. Though he looked to be in his early twenties, his teeth were brown and rotted. He smelled awful. He opened his eyes a little and took a long look at Mike. Then his eyes widened as he pulled Mike closer: "YOU AGAIN!"

Chapter Two

Outside the Old Red Barn - 4:55 A.M.
Mike recoiled from the words. "What the... what did you say?" There was no response and the man passed back into unconsciousness. Mike felt for a pulse; there was none. He looked at the girl who was dressed like a nurse. "Start CPR."

Mike started chest compressions while the nurse took care of the man's airway. Mike saw that she was new at this and visibly upset. "Ray, come here. I need you, now!"

Ray quickly moved in to take her place. When he bent down to get a better look, he recoiled from the man's odor. "Holy Christ, this guy reeks."

The young nurse stood up and walked away. Gordon grabbed the girl to comfort her and get her side of the story.

"He came out of nowhere," she said. "I didn't see him until it was too late."

The girl's cell phone rang. It was dispatch, wanting an update. Gordon took the phone from her and gave them the information they needed for the ambulance and police.

"What's the route number?" Gordon asked.

"Steinwehr Avenue," Mike said.

"We're on Steinwehr Avenue in front of an old red barn. We have one victim in critical condition. CPR is being administered."

***

The police arrived before the ambulance. They took the names of the four witnesses while waiting. The ambulance arrived and the paramedic was briefed on the patient's condition and how he was found.

Mike and Ray helped load the man into the ambulance. When the ambulance left, the policeman walked over to the young nurse. "Ma'am, you need to come with me to the precinct since you were the unfortunate one who hit the victim. You three can go."

The sun was rising when the police released Mike, Ray, and Gordon.

"Look at this," Ray said.

"Look at what?" Mike asked.

"Daylight, damn it. We left Columbus to get here early, beat the crowd, get a few hours sleep in the truck. That was the plan, and then this shit happens."

"Relax, Ray," Mike said, "the guy from the road and the girl are having a worse day then you."

"If you're gonna put it that way," Ray said.

"Have you ever seen that guy before?" Mike asked.

"Nope, not me, how about you, Gordy?"

"Not I."

"Know one thing," Ray said.

"What's that?" Mike asked.

"He was a disgusting human being. Must have the hygiene habits of a hillbilly," Ray smiled as he said it.

"I've read about hard-core authentic reenactors; they are a very strange bunch." Gordon said.

Mike and Ray exchanged looks and smiled at their inside joke about Gordon being a bookworm.

Gordon was one of those guys whose mind stored a wealth of useless information: only great if you're on a game show.

"Let's get the hell out of here." Mike said.

Mike got in the truck and shut the door. He sat, staring at the wheel, compelled to think about the young woman in white he had almost hit.

"What is it, Mike?" Gordon asked.

"Nothing. It's nothing, let's just go," Mike said.

"Of course, we may still get there and beat the crowd." Gordon said with optimism.

"Oh, shut up, you're part of the reason we're late, waiting an hour for you to get off work." Ray said.

"Excuse me, late ambo call, that's my job."

"I do my job in a timely manner," Ray said.

"Shutup, the both of you," Mike said.

It became quiet in the truck as they drove through the center of town. They made a left in the roundabout and drove west on Route 116. After a few miles, Gordon pointed at the turnoff. "We're here, Mike."

"Good, 'bout time." Mike was relieved from the long night of hell. His mind was flipping back and forth between the guy in the road and the woman in white. *Who were they?* The question plagued Mike as he made a right turn onto the dirt drive.

The traffic was heavy and dust thickened as they neared the large farm buildings. As the old truck crawled forward for almost an hour, Gordon looked out the window. "Already crowded."

"Damn, I knew it," Ray said.

"I read that the promoters held the registration to fifteen thousand reenactors this year," Gordon said.

"Looks more like twenty," Mike said.

"Yeah, just our luck, they're all here at once," Ray said.

Mike finally pulled into a parking space and the truck rocked to a stop. They got out and stretched their legs to get the kinks out again.

"The weather is supposed to be good this weekend," Gordon said.

A large, full-bearded man had parked his car next to them. He looked across his trunk at Mike. "How far did you all come in that old yellow clunker?"

"Ohio," Ray said.

"That junk, as you call it, is a 1974 Ford Bronco, and I guarantee it runs better then that piece of shit you came in," Mike said.

"Sure it does," the big man said. He laughed and walked away.

"Asshole," Mike said.

"So, this should be a great weekend, right guys?" Gordon said.

"Sure, that blowhard won't ruin our weekend," Mike said.

"Christ it's hot. Must be 90 degrees already," Ray said. He lit a cigarette with the silver flip-top Zippo his father had given him. He pulled out a candy bar and began to eat.

"You that hungry?" Mike asked.

"Yeah."

Shaking his head, Mike pulled out his great, great, grandfather's old pocket watch and set it to the truck's clock. It was a family heirloom and had been passed down four generations.

Ray looked at his watch: it was stopped. "What time is it?" He asked, and then crammed another bite of candy bar into his mouth.

"Going on ten—Christ sakes, Ray, you're three bars away from, Goddamn," Mike joked.

"That ain't right," Ray said, acting as though it hurt his feelings.

Although it was hot and the lines at the registration tent were long, they were at least moving. Mike, standing in front of Ray, noticed that some reenactors were wearing their wool uniforms buttoned to the neck already. He remembered just how uncomfortable it was to wear a wool uniform buttoned to the neck. *May as well get used to it early,* he thought.

***

For Ray, the clock ticked away very slowly. The crowd seemed to be in no hurry to sign in and find their respective companies. Other reenactors meandered around, making small talk with friends they hadn't seen since the last gathering, but to Ray, it seemed as if they had been playing the army game of hurry up and wait. The heat made the wait seem longer. "Come on, let's go. Move it along, It's hot out, you know. How hard is it to sign in, and get the hell out of the way?"

Ray, the Angry Little Man as he was known at the fire house, had started his rant.

***

Gordon was at the next table over. The Union line was always shorter, Gordon knew from past reenactments. He was also glad to be away from Ray and his bitching. He signed in with Battery A, the Fourth U.S. Light Artillery. It was written in the family's bible that his great-great-grandfather, Mortimer Smart, was a sergeant major with Cushing's battery, so Battery A was an obvious choice.

When he was done, he walked outside the tent fly and waited for his friends.

***

Behind Ray stood the large, full-bearded man from the parking lot, listening to Ray complain about the long lines.

Mike was signing in with the 9th Virginia Volunteer Infantry, Company B. Ray, standing behind Mike, was about to do the same.

"Shut your mouth," the large bearded man warned.

Ray turned to see who had spoken. He caught the dark eyes of a very large man with a black beard staring directly back at him. The man was as big as a tree, which made Ray's stature of five-foot-six seem very small. Ray recognized him from the parking lot and quickly turned away.

Mike sensed trouble and turned. He looked directly into the eyes of the large man behind Ray. The large man stared back at Mike. Mike also recognized him.

"What's you're problem?" The man asked Mike.

"You," Mike replied. He was tired from the morning craziness on the road and was in no mood for this shit.

"Get away from me before I punch you in the neck."

"Here's my neck. Go head and punch it," Mike told him.

The big man stood there. He didn't seem to know what to do.

Someone from behind the registration desk spoke out. "We'll have none of that here. You two will be asked to leave the event if you keep that up."

Mike didn't want that. "Stop complaining. Do you hear anyone else bitching?" Mike directed his comments to Ray while never turning from the large man's gaze.

Ray looked down at the ground, embarrassed.

"Apologize, Ray."

The whole crowd started to clap. They seemed delighted that someone finally shut him up. The tension between the large bearded man and Mike cooled. The big man smiled and backed off.

"I want to apologize to everyone," Ray said awkwardly, "It's just the heat and I'm very tired." Ray didn't want any trouble from the registration man or from the biggest man he had ever seen. And he didn't want Mike to get into a fight on his account.

After registration, Mike and Ray walked out from under the tent fly. Ray was looking affectionately at his commemorative medal for the 150th anniversary of the Battle of Gettysburg.

"Put it around your neck, Ray," Mike said.

"I know where it goes," Ray said.

In the recesses of his mind, Mike wanted to go back to the barn and check out the accident scene. He shrugged it off as silly. He turned and looked into the crowd. Standing there, staring directly at him was the young woman dressed in white.

Chapter Three

Outside of Registration - 10:30 A.M.
Mike saw that she was a lovely young woman, probably in her early twenties. She was standing amongst the crowd, not more then twenty feet away. She wore a period white hoop dress with a purple lace and trim accent. His eyes locked onto hers. He was captivated by her light blue eyes as she stared back into his.

She broke the trance when she turned and walked away. Mike pursued her to a tent that sold vintage clothing. Before she entered the tent, she turned, glanced at Mike and smiled, and then went inside.

Mike trailed in behind her and looked down each aisle of dresses but she was nowhere to be found. As he turned to walk out of the tent, he caught the light fragrance of lavender. He spun around, but to his dismay, she was gone. He walked outside and there stood Ray and Gordon. Excitedly he asked, "You guys see her?"

"Who?" Ray asked.

"The woman in the road we almost hit for Christ sake."

"Oh, her," Ray said.

"I just saw her again," Mike said.

"What did she want?" Ray asked.

"She didn't say, shit-ass," Mike said sarcastically.

Now having an attitude, he noticed Ray, proudly wearing his medal on the outside of his shirt.

When Ray held it up to stare at it, Mike blew him off, "It's just a token, Ray."

"Yeah, well it's my token," Ray replied.

Mike relaxed and smiled. He and Gordon exchanged looks; both knew Ray was very self-centered. Mike, who couldn't stay mad very long, moved past the incident.

"First thing, set up tents," Mike said.

"Good idea, you the man, with a plan," Gordon said.

They got back in the truck and Mike drove through the meadowland of white canvas. They headed to the Union camp first. When they pulled up to Gordon's unit, Mike stopped the truck and they got out. Mike handed Ray a bag of gear. Gordon picked up a wooden box. "Follow me Ray."

Mike brought over the tent and poles to where Gordon was setting up. Other reenactors, friends of Gordon's, were marking off the company streets and setting up tents and lean-tos. The Union camp was being set up as authentically as possible.

"Gordy, tonight about six, meet us back at registration. We'll eat together."

"Sure, Mike," Gordon said.

Mike and Ray jumped into the truck and drove back across the gravel road that ran through the center of a 495-acre farm to the Confederate side of the event.

When they got to their unit, Mike pulled over. He got out walked around and lowered the tailgate. He started pulling gear out of the back of the Bronco handing it to Ray. Several reenactors walked over to help, friends they hadn't seen since last year.

"I see that junk wagon still gets you here," one said.

"Hey, watch what you say about my truck," Mike said.

They all laughed. They caught up on all the latest news, the weekend's schedule for the 150$^{th.}$ They talked about the weather and the state of the 9th regiment, one of five regiments of Armistead's Brigade, part of Pickett's division, of Longstreet's II Corps.

"Any officers show up yet?" Mike asked one of the guys.

"Only the Corporal, who's busy getting directions from the Major on how they want us to set up the company street," he said.

The Corporal, dressed in butternut, slowly walked back, shaking his head. He was sporting a reddish mustache and goatee. He noticed the guys waiting patiently for direction.

"What's the verdict, Chip?" Mike asked.

"Hey Mike, good to see ya. I guess I'll just have to make an executive decision," he said. "Since the Major doesn't know how each company will set up. He told me he leaves that to the ranking officer of each company to decide. Since I'm the only one here with stripes, here's where we'll set up."

"I like a man who can make a decision, 'lead, follow, or get out of the way,' is the saying," Mike said with a big smile on his face.

Then they all got busy setting up camp. Mike pitched his discolored, mildew-riddled, canvas dog tent, which fastened to the ground with steel spikes made exactly like the originals.

Afterwards, Mike and Ray stood around talking with the others about the last reenactment and how cool it would have been to have lived back in that time period.

"I would gladly live back during the 1860's. I think it would be great, an easier, simpler way of life," Chip said.

"Oh, hell no, no way I'm giving up my push button world. I can just push a button and get ice," Mike said.

"But just think how simple life was back then," Chip said.

"Don't get me wrong, I'd like to visit, maybe for a week or two, but I would want to get back home after that," Mike said.

"Pickett's Charge, now that would be cool. I would kick some Yankee ass at the Angle," Ray said.

"You'll get your chance. The sponsors built the rock wall complete with the Union's Angle and they placed forty cannons there," Corporal Chip said. "They also have some surprises in store for us this weekend."

"Oh yeah, like what?" Mike asked.

"Well, all I can tell ya is that they planned the 150th like a tactical. The event starts at six. After that, we are at war and all the rules of war apply," Chip advised.

"Sounds like my kind of fun," Mike said.

Mike looked out across the field. The Confederate camp looked like an ocean of white, tents as far as the eye could see. Pick-up trucks were hauling horse trailers, cannons with caissons, and period wagons, to place them around camp to complete the look of the era. And then someone's cell phone ring tone sounded, breaking the mood. Embarrassed about the modern distraction, a reenactor got up and answered his phone.

"Will ya'll just please leave your cell phones in your cars?" Corporal Chip requested.

Then a car pulled up and the occupant hollered, "Where's the 14th Virginia setting up?" It was the same large man, hanging a field map out the driver's side window.

Mike walked over to the driver. "Didn't I get enough of you at registration?"

"The way I remember it was, you and your loudmouth buddy almost got us thrown out. I'll go ask someone else."

"You do that," Mike said.

The large man threw the map on the passenger seat put, the car in gear, and pealed out.

Mike walked over to Ray.

"Was that who I think it was?"

"Yeah, don't worry about him."

"Easy for you to say," Ray mumbled.

Mike paid no attention to him and moved on. "Since this is your first time in the field, watch and learn, Ray. Let's get our bunks ready for tonight."

Mike tore apart the bail of straw and used it as bedding inside the tent. He threw a gum blanket on top to keep out the ground moisture. His gray wool blanket acted as a bedroll to complete his bunk.

Mike sat on the ground next to the tent, which provided some privacy. He slipped on his reproduction socks and his light gray wool pants. Pulled up his white linen suspenders and looked over at Ray, who was wearing his butternut paints and jacket over a white shirt.

Mike finished his look with a brown plaid shirt and a gray vest. Then he slipped on his four-button fatigue jacket to complete his Virginia grays. He looked over at Ray slipping his Brogans over modern socks.

"You don't have period socks?" Mike asked.

"You're lucky I have Brogans, at 110 dollars a pair. Sorry to disappoint," Ray said.

Mike placed his gray forage cap on his head. He smiled and said, "Fresh fish."

Ray threw on his brown slouch hat. "Fresh fish this."

Mike knelt down into the tent. He positioned his and Ray's leather gear, which consisted of a cartridge box, cap pouch, and a seven-rivet scabbard with bayonet on two black leather belts, under the blanket. He set their reproduction 1863 two band percussion Enfield rifles beside them. Mike hoped that their stuff would be safe and out of sight from wandering eyes.

After a long day of setting up camp, Mike and Ray were ready to go. They walked over to Chip and the boys who were still reminiscing about past reenactments that sounded real and deadly.

The first sergeant walked up to the group.

"Get those buggies out of camp." It was the third time that the first sergeant had told everyone to move their vehicles.

"Let's go, Ray. Don't forget your haversack and canteen. It's always good to have water and a haversack in case you buy something."

They walked over to the truck and Mike leaped in. "You coming?"

Ray didn't hesitate. Mike had left him before, so he quickly jumped in the truck.

They drove back to the parking lot, kicking up dust as they went. Mike found a nice spot and pulled in.

They walked back toward registration, where they waited for Gordon by a split rail fence.

A warm breeze blew and the straw that the reenactors used for bedding drifted across the picturesque farmland. Women and children dressed in period clothing walked up and down the sides of the dirt road as cars and trucks passed. Young boys played with stick rifles as little girls rolled large wooden hoops along the grass.

Ray shook out another Camel and lit up. "What's the time?" He asked.

Mike pulled out his antique pocket watch and looked at the hands. "Six-thirty, farb."

"Farb? Who you calling a farb?"

"You! Cigarettes, Zippo lighter, candy bars, you're a disgrace," Mike said. "And put that damn commemorative medal under your shirt."

"Okay, okay," Ray said defensively. "For your information, some modern comforts from home allow for a more pleasurable reenacting experience," he said. Ray took a drag and looked around. "Where the hell is Gordy? He needs to get his head straight. Why does he always have to be different? If he'd join the Confederacy as I did, we wouldn't have to wait for him."

"He's independent, besides, his great-great-grandfather was a sergeant major with Cushing's Battery, remember?"

"Well, then I'm sure someone in my family fought for the South," Ray snapped.

Mike smiled. "You just like the Confederate flag on your t-shirt, Ray."

"It's a nice looking flag," Ray said as a big smile grew on his face. "So I guess we'll just stand here and wait for Gordon. Hell, why not? We waited an hour for him to get off work, so why not wait for him to go to supper? I feel like this is what we do now, wait on Gordon."

"Don't start with that shit, Ray. It will take a while for your ass to starve to death. I'm sure you have plenty of Snickers bars in your haversack."

Ray's eyes blinked in his round face. He gave Mike that you-hurt-my-feelings look and then said, "I do have feelings, you know, even if they are little itty-bitty ones." He smiled. Mike smiled back; he liked busting on Ray, knowing he'd take it well.

"It will be dark before he gets here. I'm not waiting any longer," Ray declared. "Let's just go. He can meet us there."

"Daylight savings time, Ray, hell, won't be dark until after nine. The plan is we came together, we eat together, got it?"

"Okay. Okay, you and your plans. And for your information, my Snickers bars are for dessert." Ray folded his arms with an innocent look on his face. "What if we missed him?" Ray asked. "What if we were late? He might have come and gone. He might be up there waiting for us right now."

"Not Gordon. You know how he is, a man of his word," Mike said.

Just then, Gordon appeared on the horizon. Coming their way, he wore a warm smile on his face. His long neck made his blue shell jacket with red trim look a bit small. The red trimmed kepi on his head was tilted forward, almost touching his wire-rimmed glasses. In the glow of the sunlight behind him, he looked like an authentic artillery gunner marching over the hill.

"Here comes the geek now, late as usual," Ray said.

"Oh please, tell me you missed me?" Gordon said with a smile as he walked up.

"What took so long?" Ray asked.

"It's quite difficult to leave old friends you haven't seen for such a long time."

"What, last year?" Ray said. "Come on, let's eat."

"We better go before Ray passes out," Mike said.

They started to walk towards Sutler's Row.

"I heard the weather forecast," Gordon said.

"Beautiful, all weekend."

Chapter Four

Sutler's Row - 7:16 P.M.

Mike, Ray, and Gordon walked the dusty gravel road toward the main entrance. There, the vendors lined up across from one another creating a street known as Sutler's Row. They were convenient to all who entered the event, reenactors as well as the general public.

Under reproduction white canvas tents and flys, the vendors sold their wares. Mike's senses tingled with the smells of pit beef and onions. There were turkey legs cooking over the open grills.

Since this was his last chance to eat a half-decent meal before they got stuck back at camp eating cabbage and ham stew, Mike ordered the pit beef and french fries.

Ray ordered the same, but Gordon eyed the roasted turkey legs and bought one of them instead. After getting their food, they moved to a large tent fly that had been erected for dining accommodations. They found a seat with a group of four other Confederate soldiers.

Ray was suddenly distressed when he saw who was sitting at the other end of the same picnic table: the large bearded man from registration.

It was too late to go to a different table, besides the area was already crowded. And he saw that Mike and Gordon had already sat down and had begun to eat. Ray slowly took a seat beside Mike.

"Mike, look to your left front. It's Tree Man," Ray whispered, nicknaming the man.

"Who?" Mike asked.

"Tree Man, the big guy from registration," Ray strained to keep his voice low.

"So what? Eat your roast beef," Mike said.

Seeing that Mike wasn't worried, Ray began to relax.

"How's your turkey leg, Gordy?" Mike asked.

"Hey you, the one that looks like a boar without tusks," someone interrupted. "I know you." He pointed at Ray. "Hey fellows, that's the complainer from registration. Don't lie, you know who you are."

Ray sank in his chair, more embarrassed then scared, as his face blushed red. Tree Man shifted closer to him and Ray became nervous. "I see you made it through registration. Feel better now?" The large man maintained a stern look.

"Yes, well... I'm better now," Ray muttered, not knowing what else to say.

Mike listened to every word but didn't move. He had run-ins with obnoxious loudmouths before and knew that, in the end, they all back down. He kept right on eating.

The large man relaxed his gaze. He seemed to have gotten what he wanted: Ray scared. "Did you hear about that reenactor getting hit by a car this morning?"

"Yes, we were there and the guy acted like he knew Mike," Ray said, glad to get the attention off him and onto Mike.

"You guys were there?" Tree Man asked with excitement in his voice.

"What about it?" Mike asked coldly.

"Well, you gonna tell us?"

"The guy was hit by a car, what else you need to know?" Mike said matter of fact.

The large man stood up at the table and took a step toward Mike. Mike rose and stared directly at him, waiting for any reason to strike and aggression was as good as any other reason.

The man smirked, reached down into his cooler and pulled out a bottle of National Bohemian, sat back down, and opened it. After a long gulp, he placed the beer on the table. "Go on, I want to hear about the part where he knows you."

He drank his beer right in front of everyone, showing no fear of breaking the rules. Gordon shook his head in disbelief.

A smile came across Mike's face; he just had to ask. "Who are you anyway?"

"Treble, Thomas Treble, 14th Virginia."

Gordon leaned over, "Nice to make your acquaintance."

"You don't care who you sit with, do ya?" Tom said.

"What's that mean?" Mike asked.

"He's a Yankee man, don't ya see?"

"So what," Mike said.

"Never mind, is somebody going to tell us what happened this morning?" Tom asked.

Mike started to tell the tale when Gordon put his hand out and stopped him. "Let the Yankee tell it, Mike."

Mike relaxed and sat back down. "All yours."

"Well Tom, it was about five this morning when a reenactor was hit by a car. We were first on the scene and Mike here rendered medical aid. Then all of a sudden, the guy grabbed his shirt and pulled him to his face and said, *'you again'*."

"Wow, so did you know him?" Tom asked Mike.

"No, I never saw him before," Mike said.

"Now that's messed up. Maybe he knew you from past reenactments?" Tom asked.

"Maybe, who knows... and who cares? Can we change the subject now?" Mike said hotly.

"Change the subject?" Tom said.

"That's what I said, don't make me sorry," Mike said, becoming agitated.

"The ambulance came and hauled him away, end of story," Gordon said.

"Seems to me some people just don't know when to give up their first person impression," Tom said with a smile.

Gordon smiled. "Did you guys ever hear about the story of lost gold in Gettysburg?" Gordon asked.

"That's more like it," Mike relaxed.

"Okay, I'm good with that," Tom said.

"There is an intriguing story of lost Confederate gold," Gordon said.

Ray stopped eating. "You've got my attention."

"Twenty-dollar gold pieces, double eagles, were stolen from General Jeb Stuart's strong box that he pilfered during his invasion of the north and was going to take them back to Richmond for the war effort-"

"Pilfered my ass," Tom interrupted. "Took back only what was stolen in the first place. Payback is hell."

"Well, okay... the point is that the last time anyone saw the gold was right here, before the battle of Gettysburg. It was never recovered. Maybe the gold is still here somewhere, just waiting to be found," Gordon said.

"Yeah right, buried next to Hoffa." Tom said.

The whole table started to laugh. Ray went back to eating. Gordon watched Ray and waited for him to stuff his mouth with roast beef. "What do you think?" Gordon timed the question perfectly. Ray shrugged his shoulders, and then with his mouth full blurted out, "Anything's possible," spitting his food everywhere.

"Christ Ray, do you have spit your food when you talk?" Mike said wiping the food off his coat.

"I'm hungry," Ray said spitting more food.

"You don't have to be a pig about it," Mike said.

Gordon smiled watching Ray's reaction.

"Think somebody found it?" Ray asked as he swallowed.

"All the looking that has been done around here, someone would have found it long before now." Mike said.

"Ha, Ha, Ha...you boys sure do have some imagination!" Laughing, Tom slammed the empty beer bottle on the table. His buddies all joined in on Tom's laughter.

"Mike, you look like the backwoodsman type," Tom noted.

"And you look like Blackbeard the Pirate," Mike said with a smile.

Tom leaned back into his chair and laughed. "I guess I deserve that one." He laughed some more then rubbed his full belly with both hands. "I feel like a fat tick on a dog's back." He barked out another laugh. He stood to leave and said, "Let's go." He looked at Mike, and then at Ray and Gordon. "You boys want a Natty Boh to get you started for the weekend?"

"No, thanks, we have our own back at camp," Mike said.

"Well then, we're gonna head back now. See ya on the battlefield tomorrow. You fellows have a good night." Then he looked at Mike and added, "Especially you, badass."

"See ya in my sights," Mike said.

"Accidents happen," Tom said.

"That shit works both ways," Mike told him.

Tom stared at Mike for a while, and then picked up one end of the cooler and walked away with the others toward their camp.

"What did he mean by that?" Ray asked.

Mike got up from the table. "Don't worry about it. He's an asshole."

"I see you still know how to influence people and make friends," Gordon said.

"I could have used a beer, Mike," Ray said.

"You don't need a beer added to that gut," Mike said.

"But Mike, it was a Natty Boh."

"Yeah, the worst beer on the planet if you ask me," Gordon said.

"Who asked ya?" Ray said.

Mike stretched his arms over his head and gave an audible yawn. Then he reached into his vest and pulled out his pocket watch. "Near eight, let's take a walk."

Ray got up, brushing crumbs off his shirt as he went. He pulled out his smokes and put one in his mouth. He flipped open the lid of his Zippo with one hand and lit the cigarette. Slipping the lighter back in his pants pocket, Ray opened his haversack and pulled out a half melted candy bar and shoved it in his mouth, getting chocolate all over his fingers and lips.

Mike looked at him again with disappointment. "I see that my job this weekend is to teach you how not to be a farb."

"Just because I have some modern comforts from home, doesn't make me a farb."

Gordon gave Ray a friendly smile. "Yeah, pretty much, it does."

"Who cares what you two think, anyway? Just tell me where we're going."

"To my truck," Mike said.
"Why?" Ray asked.
"We're going to the barn."
"The barn?" Gordon had forgotten all about the barn.

Mike had gotten the sudden urge to go to the barn. "I've wanted to look around it all day. Let's go before the sun goes down."

"While we're there maybe we can look for the gold," Ray said.

Chapter Five

Reenactors Parking lot - 8:07 P.M.

Mike, along with Ray and Gordon, climbed back into the Bronco and drove back through the town of Gettysburg. Mike hung a left and drove down Steinwehr Avenue. He stopped the truck along the road a few yards north of the barn.

They walked over to the front of the big red barn. Looking out across the field opposite the barn, Mike could see where the Confederates marched across the open field. "Pickett's Charge," Mike muttered.

"Amazing," Gordon said.

"What?" Ray asked.

"The chaos and confusion that must have ensued as the Confederate soldiers made their last desperate effort to overwhelm the Union forces," Gordon said. "So many lives lost: fathers, sons, and brothers."

Mike understood the reason why so many reenactors gathered here every year.

"Ever have a reenactor's moment, Mike?" Gordon asked.

Mike didn't respond.

"You know, when everything feels real?" Gordon said.

"No, can't say that I have," Mike finally said.

"Once, I did, just for a second," Gordon said. "It was in the heat of battle, the rebs were storming our lines, overrunning our guns. Hand to hand combat. At that precise moment, I lost myself, just for a few seconds. It actually felt real. Now that's a cool feeling."

"Right up to the time you realized no one was getting killed," Mike said.

"No, right up to the time I looked up from the book," Gordon smiled when he said it.

Ray laughed.

"There's way too many modern distractions for me," Mike said.

"Well, Mike, maybe this will be your weekend," Ray said.

Mike saw that the old barn was a two-story wood frame structure with two large doors in the front, facing the road. He noticed a side door on the right side.

Mike walked over to the door and found it unlocked. "Hummm."

"What is it, Mike?" Ray asked.

"Let's see what's behind door number one," Mike said.

"Wait-" Gordon warned.

But before he could say more, Mike and Ray had slipped inside. Cautiously, Gordon looked in through the dark opening, still hesitant. With another breath, he walked through the door.

Once inside, Gordon saw the shadows of his friends wandering around the barn. "Does the term breaking and entering mean anything to you two?" He asked.

"Hello, is anybody in here?" Mike called out.

"Expecting someone?" Ray asked.

"See, Gordy, no one's here, relax," Mike said.

Ray began to explore the barn. The light from outside was shining through the uneven openings in the sideboards and through the cracks in the roof. Other than dirt, dust, and cobwebs that covered the large wooden structures, the barn was completely empty.

"Do you guys smell that?" Mike asked.

Ray sniffed at the air and paused. "Smell what?"

"Smells like something's dead," Mike said looking up at the hayloft.

"I never cared much for the smell of Eau de Barn," Mike smiled and continued to the hayloft. He came to an old wooden ladder and noticed that the plank flooring was pulling up in places leaving holes just the right size for ankle breakers.

"Be careful, there are holes in the floor," Mike said.

Mike began to climb the ladder to the hayloft.

"Be careful," warned Gordon, "Those rungs have to be over a hundred years old and it doesn't appear that the Gettysburg Restoration Committee had included this little beauty in their renovation plans."

Mike paid no attention and climbed to the top and looked across the floor covered with hay. As his eyes adjusted to the darkness, he saw a large figure in the corner. "Is that an animal?" Mike wondered aloud. "Hey guys, check this out."

Drawn by curiosity, Mike crawled toward the dark figure. Green flies were everywhere. As Mike got closer, the smell of decaying flesh grew stronger. There was a floor board leaning against a post. He stopped. He made out the figure next to the board.

Ray climbed the wooden ladder while Gordon grabbed a lantern before starting his climb.

"What is it, Mike?" Ray asked.

"Let me see your lighter, Ray."

Ray was swatting at the flies trying to keep them out of his face. "Sure, now my lighter comes in handy," Ray joked. He took out his Zippo and handed it to Mike.

"Wait, Mike. Here's a lantern," Gordon said crawling over. He handed the lantern to Mike, who lit it. The light glowed, revealing the figure to the others.

"Oh shit, that's a dead guy," Ray said.

"We should check and make sure," Gordon suggested.

"That smell makes me sure enough," Mike said.

Gordon started to crawl to the man when Mike grabbed him. "What do you think you're doing?"

"I'm going to check him."

"He's dead and that's all there is to it. Don't disturb anything," Mike warned while tightening his grip on Gordon.

"We need to tell the police right away," Gordon said as he struggled with Mike.

"No, we don't, do you want to be answering questions the rest of the weekend? Miss out on the biggest reenactment of your life?" Mike was holding him tight.

"No, I don't, but–"

"Then shut up about the police," Mike said. Then he saw the fear on Gordon's face. "Look, after the weekend we'll all go to the police and tell them all about it."

Gordon eased up a bit. "Okay, okay, we'll play it your way this time." Gordon brushed off Mike's grip. "You don't have to get so rough with me."

Mike noticed a hole in the floor. "This must be where the floorboard came from." He shined the light down into it. It was a hollowed out joist. He looked closer. Then he pulled out a small box from its resting place. "Look what I got."

Gordon, trying to cool down and relax, looked at the box. "It's a tinderbox."

"A what?" Ray asked, holding his nose and looking befuddled.

Gordon composed himself, swatted at the green flies, and then began. "Historically speaking, a tinderbox is a small tin container that kept your tinder dry, either "charcloth" or straw. It usually contained a piece of flint rock and a firesteel for striking the spark."

Ray and Mike exchanged looks and smiled.

"After matches, lucifers, as they were called, came into use, the tinderbox became a museum piece."

"Where do you come up with this stuff?" Ray said nasally, still holding his nose.

Mike smiled then opened the box and took out a piece of parchment paper. He held it in the light and saw the words *Tempus Fugit* written in cursive along the fold. "What does this look like to you, Gordy?"

Gordon looked it over for a moment. "It's Latin. It means 'time flies.'" Gordon handed the rolled paper back to Mike.

"Time flies, huh?" Mike muttered.

"Yeah well, tempus fugit, when you're having fun, right guys?" Ray joked.

Mike unfolded the paper, revealing a written inscription. "What do you make of this?"

Gordon tried to see what was written and motioned for more light. Before he read the words he noticed that something was carved onto the lid of the tinderbox.

"That's a pentagram." Gordon said.

"Like the devil's pentagram... like, this is some kind of devil box?" Ray said.

"Originally, the pentagram was a sign of purity. It was created by ancient religions that practiced the worship of many gods."

"Here we go again," whispered Ray.

"Christianity," Gordon continued, "began to associate this old pure symbol with evil, sickness, and the devil. They hoped it would deter the villagers from practicing the beliefs of their ancestors."

"So it is the devil's box!" exclaimed Ray.

Ray noticed a small hourglass in the box. He picked it up and began to play with it. "I knew I'd fine something cool."

Gordon knew it wasn't worth explaining again so he looked at Mike and asked, "So what do you want to do now?"

"Read the parchment," Mike said.

Gordon unrolled the parchment, adjusted the light and said, "The poem."

"What?" Mike asked.

"The inscription is a poem," Gordon explained.

"So what?" Mike said. "Just read it."

Gordon began to read. Ray, fiddling with the hourglass, turned it over and absentmindedly sat it down to listen. The white crystals started to fall, sparkling as they went. No one noticed.

> *"Many paths through centuries fall-*
> *If change is what you seek.*
> *Illumination shines true for all-*
> *Fulfillment for the meek."*

The last grain of white sand fell and the lantern flickered and went out.

"Someone turn on the lights," Mike said.

"What the hell was that all about?" Ray asked, no longer holding his nose.

"Sounds like some kind of spell," Gordon said.

"Spell, huh... let's get the hell outta here. I don't need this witchcraft devil bullshit," Ray said.

"Settle down, Ray, and hand me your lighter again to light this lamp," Mike said.

Mike lit the lantern. "Ray, you're not holding your nose." The flies were gone. The rotten odor was gone also. Mike looked around. "Where's the body?"

Gordon looked to where the man's body had been lying. "Where did it go?"

"Ooohh shiii... I'm outta here!" Ray said. "I'll see you back at the truck."

Ray made his way toward the ladder and began to climb down.

"Let's put everything back the way we found it." Gordon insisted.

"Yeah, put the stuff back in the box and place it in the floor," Mike said. "Don't forget to put the floorboard back and cover it with straw. I'm going after Ray and calm his ass down."

As Gordon put things back, Mike scurried over to the ladder trying to catch up with Ray.

Ray was at a full gallop when he hit the small wooden table in the middle of the floor. He hit it with full force, knocking it over, sending both him and the table crashing to the floor.

Hearing the crash, Mike came running and found Ray sprawled out on the floor. Mike picked up the table and placed it right side up.

"Where the hell did that come from?" Mike asked as he helped Ray to his feet. "Are you okay?"

Gordon walked over with the lantern and saw a bench. "You missed this one, Ray," Gordon said, shaking his head in amusement. He placed the lantern on the table.

"How did we miss all this? I could swear it wasn't here before, but it must have been," Gordon said scratching his head.

"I got to get the hell out of here," Ray said and bolted for the door.

Mike went after him, but Ray was gone. Gordon joined Mike out side the barn. "Where'd he go?"

"Halfway home, the way he was running," Mike said.

Suddenly, there was a scream in the distance.

Chapter Six

The Open Field across from the Barn - 9:01 P.M.

It was a familiar, angry scream that Mike knew all too well. "Ray!" Mike yelled. He took off toward the screech. Gordon was close behind. Mike found Ray sprawled out on the ground. Ray was rolling around trying to get away from whatever he fell over.

"Ray, you alright?" Mike asked.

Ray brushing himself off stood up. "What the hell is that?"

"What ever it is, it stinks," Mike said.

Guarding his nose Gordon remarked, "I can't see real well, but it looks like a dead animal."

"It's a cow!" Mike exclaimed.

"What the hell is a dead cow doing out here?" Gordon asked.

"Maybe she had a heart attack and dropped dead," Mike jested.

"Let's get going," Ray begged. "Christ, I'm ready to go home and forget this whole weekend." Ray was shaking, trying to light a cigarette.

"Calm down, you're okay now," Mike told him, looking at his uneasiness.

Ray finally lit his cigarette and took a long drag.

"Sure, I'm cool, dead people disappearing and stuff, hey, I'm cool with that," Ray said as he took another long drag and looked into the night.

"Look," Gordon said, "we'll report what we saw to the authorities and let them deal with finding the body. There has to be a perfectly good explanation for all this. Someone is playing a trick on us I bet."

"Nice trick," Ray said exhaling a cloud of smoke.

"Sure got dark fast," Mike said trying to see the hands on his antique pocket watch.

"What happened to daylight savings?" Ray asked.

"Good point, it's only nine," Mike said.

"Clouds came in," Gordon said.

"Thought you said the forecast was clear skies this whole weekend," Ray said.

"Guess I was wrong," Gordon mumbled, "Should we go back to the barn and blow out the lantern?"

"Oh, hell no, I'm not going back into Voodoo Central," Ray said.

Mike laughed. In the distance Mike thought he heard reenactors chopping wood. "Hear that?" A moment later he heard the sound of musket fire. "That sounded close," Mike said.

"It sounded like it came from Culp's Hill. Is there a tactical we don't know about?" Gordon asked.

"Probably a demonstration," Ray said.

"They don't allow shooting," Mike remembered.

"Let's get back to the truck," Ray suggested.

"Sounds like a plan," Mike said.

"Let's go to the authorities," Gordon advised.

"What do you suggest we tell them, the dead can disappear?"

"I'm with Mike, we should keep our mouths shut," Ray said and took another drag.

"You promised," Gordon mentioned.

"You're the one big on promises."

Mike started to walk back toward the truck. Ray wiped his coat, grumbling about the cow shit all over him.

"I'm going to the barn," Gordon said.

"Why?" Mike asked.

"We left the lantern lit."

"Fine. Lead the way," Mike said.

Gordon walked toward the barn. When Mike turned, he saw out the corner of his eye, the woman in white: the same girl from the road. She was standing in the middle of the field in the direction of Seminary Ridge. "Stop, do you guys see her," Mike whispered. He looked and Gordon was too far to hear.

"Too dark," Ray said.

"Come with me." Mike had a sudden impulse to go to her.

"What about Gordy?"

"He'll be alright until we get back."

"Yeah, his turn to wait on us," Ray said taking great delight in the thought.

Every time Mike approached the woman, she seemed to move farther away. He'd get closer, she'd move farther back. She did this until Mike didn't see her anymore. But he did see a glow in the distance. "Is that campfires?"

Ray looked toward the hillside. He saw the glows but couldn't tell if it was a campfire. "Beats the shit out of me, let's go back."

Mike turned to walk back to the truck when, suddenly, out of the dark, a shot cracked the silence. Mike and Ray both ducked for cover. "What the hell?" Mike shouted.

Then there was a second shot. Mike heard the bullet hit the ground a few feet away. Mike and Ray hit the ground.

"Advance, one, with the countersign," said a southern voice.

Mike looked up. "What the hell are you doing?"

"Advance and be recognized, or I'll shoot ya."

"Okay, okay, don't shoot. I'm unarmed." Mike stood up and approached the bush where the shots came from. In the meantime, Ray laid there and waited. When Mike got within six paces of the bush, the voice warned. "Halt, and give the countersign."

"What the hell you talking about? We're with the Ninth Virginia."

"How many are ya?" The voice from the bush asked.

"Two," Mike said.

"Where the other?" The voice said with a southern drawl.

Ray stood up. "You're not going to shoot me, are you?" And then he walked over next to Mike.

Then the Corporal of the Guard came up. "What's all the commotion?" The corporal wasn't in the best of moods after being disturbed by gunshots. "Report."

Two boys, one about the age of sixteen and the other about fourteen, emerged from the cover of the brushes. They were bearing .57 caliber Enfield rifles, aiming them at Mike and Ray.

Even though they were young, they had the faces of hardened warriors. Dirt stained their faces with black powder rubbed around the mouth areas. Their uniforms were mere rags held together by string.

"What is this, *Angels with Dirty Faces*? Hell, you're only kids for Christ sake," Ray said.

"Arms - Port," the corporal ordered.

The boys lowered their muskets. The sergeant of the guard got there with a guard of four men. "Whatta-got?"

The younger boy spoke up nervously. "These two fellows say they're with the 9th Virginia, but we don't recognize them and they don't know the countersign."

"Why don't you know the countersign?" The sergeant asked. As he waited for an answer, he scanned them for any immediate threat.

Ray was tired, and annoyed. "Look, I got dead cow all over me. I just want to go back to my tent and get some sleep. I don't care about your damn countersign!"

"We're just out taking a walk. We didn't know the event started already," Mike told him.

Ray leaned toward the younger boy and in a childlike voice whispered, "We need to get back so that we can play the game, too."

The older boy's face lit up in anger. "Ya'll out here with no guns, no lanterns, nothin, and to you it's a game."

"We left them back in camp," Ray didn't know what else to say. He didn't realize they would be so mad.

"Ya'll took a heck of a chance out there in no man's land," the older boy shook his head. "Mighty stupid."

"Where ya'll from?" The sergeant asked, noticing their accent.

"Ohio, but we joined the South, lost cause and all that," Mike said.

"Whatcha talkin 'bout, lost cause?" the older boy asked angrily.

Mike laughed, then quickly stopped and suppressed the urge. The four men standing guard looked fidgety.

"Think this is funny, do ya? I don't know ya, so I guess I got to arrest ya. corporal, arrest these two," the sergeant ordered.

The guard came over with iron handcuffs. Mike straightened up and in a matter-of-fact way said, "This is park property."

"Park property?" The sergeant, not knowing exactly what he meant by that, scratched his head and looked at the corporal for an answer. The corporal just shrugged his shoulders.

"Mike, do you think this is one of the surprises they were talking about earlier?" Ray asked.

"Look this is just a formality. We won't put the irons on ya'll so as long as you behave yourself. You can just walk with the escort back to the reserve."

"What about my truck?" Mike asked.

"What the hell ya talking 'bout?"

Mike figured that the tactical had started and that they were strangely deep into first person. So he patiently walked with the guard. The sergeant and corporal lead the detail back to support, leaving the two boys still on sentry duty.

After reaching support, which was a half mile farther in the wrong direction, Mike saw that there were about 30 men that made up the unit.

Mike watched as the guard was changed out. The corporal and his guard were relieved. The new guard and the sergeant were ready to move out.

"May I ask a question, sir?" Mike interrupted.

"What is it?" The sergeant said.

"Who the hell are you people?"

"Scuse me?"

"What the hell is all this doing on park property?"

The corporal leaned toward the sergeant. "He has a fixation 'bout park property,"

"Noticed," the sergeant said. "Me'n mah boys will take ya'll back to the reserve."

"But my truck is back that way," Mike said and pointed in the other direction.

"Yeah, well, the reserve is that way," the sergeant pointed in the opposite direction.

"This is bullshit and you know it," Mike said.

"Best shut your mouf, boy, and come with us," the sergeant cautioned him.

Then Mike heard a musket shot from the direction where they had left Gordon and became alarmed. "What was that?"

"What's going on, Mike?" Ray asked, getting nervous.

"Easy, Ray, do what they say." Mike didn't want to make things worse. He decided to make the best of a bad situation. Mike reluctantly went with the guard. He hoped that Gordon would be alright.

The sergeant and a squad of six men walked the pair up and over Seminary Ridge. They walked through the woods and down into the valley, tin cups clanking as they went.

"My feet hurt," Ray said.

"Where we going?" Mike asked the sergeant.

"Just over yondah."

They reached another tree line. Mike thought he could hear water running. *Must be a stream.*

"How much farther?" Ray asked.

"Back'a that outcroppin."

When the squad reached the clearing, Mike saw a group of soldiers double the size of the last group. They were bivouac in the trees. *Where did all these guys come from?*

They were taken to the captain of a company of skirmishers. He was sitting at a small fire chewing tobacco when he spit black juice into the fire. The captain rose and turned around, facing them. "Whada-we have here?"

"Evenin' captain, found these two wandering around in no man's land."

"Dang, why ya'll out yondah?" The captain asked.

Mike saw that the captain had a command presence about him, but didn't care; he had had enough. "Are we done? I would like to go back to my truck now."

"Sergeant, do I detect a 'tude?"

"Yessir, a bad 'tude. But one thing seemed funny, they had no weapons."

"In no man's land? Not the brightest candle in the tent, are they sergeant?" The captain thought a moment. "Ever hear of the enemy infiltrating the line without being armed?

"No sir, can't say that I have."

"They don't seem dangerous. We know they're dang idiots, but not dangerous. You boys promise not to do anything stupid and we won't tie you to a tree."

"We just want to leave," Mike said.

"You know we can't let you do that," the captain said.

Mike noticed the captain tapping the handle of his revolver. *Is it possible they're rogue Confederate reenactors? Will they harm us?* Mike worried more about Ray and decided to go along and see where it took them. "Okay, we'll play it your way, for now."

The captain turned his gaze upon Ray. "You're a stout little fellow."

Ray didn't know what to say, so he said nothing.

"How'd you get so well fed?" The captain asked.

Ray still didn't answer.

"Look, we're out 'bout two miles 'head of Longstreet's II Corps. They should be here in the morning. If'n you're really with the ninth, like you say, just wait 'til morning and things will get straight then."

"Why can't you just let us go?" Mike asked.

"Can't go wandering out here in the dark," the captain said. He turned to the sergeant. "Sergeant, get them a blanket." He turned back to Mike. "You can roll up over there." The captain pointed at a lean-two.

"Oh, hell no!" Ray said. He was terrified to sleep out under the stars with no tent.

"I'll be, he does talk. Givin' the situation, I don't think you boys have a choice." The captain's tone was very matter-of-fact.

The sergeant came back with two blankets. He handed one to each.

"This is ridiculous," Ray said.

"Come on, Ray, just one night."

Ray wrapped the blanket around his body, fell to the ground, and then rolled to the lean-two. Mike, already there, was wondering who these guys were and what they wanted. He was listening to the cracking of the fire when he heard a familiar sound. "You hear horses?"

"Yeah, but what are we going to do, Mike?"

"We need to get away from these clowns, but the captain is right about one thing, we can't do it in the dark."

"Then when?"

"First light."

"What's all that rumbling about? Get some shut-eye," the captain told them.

"Son-of-a-bitch, probably a high school janitor in the real world," Ray said.

Mike giggled.

"Told you to get some sleep. Won't tell ya again," the captain growled.

Mike quieted down. The glow of the remaining embers was dying out.

***

Meanwhile, back at the outpost where the two young sentries were, the excitement was over and the older boy relaxed so he could think a bit clearer. "Taking a walk... in no man's land... dang, what the hell were they thinking?"

The younger boy scratched his head in befuddlement. "What did he mean when he said he didn't know the eee-vent started?"

The older boy shrugged his shoulders and said, "Don't rightly know, the dumb bastards even think it's a game."

Chapter Seven

Outside the Old Red Barn - 9:13 P.M.

Gordon walked toward the barn. The night was darker than usual. He looked ahead for light, but there were no street lights. He turned around for Mike and Ray; they were gone, too. He was more concerned about the lit lantern in the barn. He shrugged his shoulders and kept walking, figuring they would be waiting for him at the truck.

He kept his eyes focused down at the ground so as not to trip in the tall grass. When he got to Emmittsburg Road, he saw that it was dirt.

Two sentinels on the Union front line stepped in front of him, their .58 caliber Springfield rifles pointed directly at him. "Advance and be recognized."

Gordon wasn't paying attention and was confused by the question. He wondered who these scraggy looking reenactors in blue were and why they had stopped him. He waved them off and started to walk around them. A shot rang out. One of the soldiers fired his musket over Gordon's head. The concussion was enough to make Gordon crouch down in pain, holding his left ear.

"What the hell is wrong with you?" Gordon yelled.

"You didn't stop and I'm still waiting on the countersign," the soldier shouted.

"Is it asshole?" Gordon yelled holding his ear.

Just then, a corporal ran over. Panting from the run over he asked, "What's going on here?"

"We found this... gentleman walking the field outside our lines. We challenged him for the countersign and he didn't know it."

The corporal caught his breath. "Sergeant of the guard," he shouted.

Gordon began to move away from the strange men. They were taking this reenactment shit way too far. Then he remembered that this was a tactical event and these guys were acting in first person. "You're messing with me and I don't like it," Gordon said as he continued to back away.

The two men grabbed his arm to restrain him. Gordon broke free and tried to run toward the truck where he thought Mike and Ray were. As he turned, he ran into two other soldiers standing at port arms. One soldier, with the butt of his rifle, knocked Gordon to the ground. Four more soldiers then quickly surrounded him and leveled their rifles directly at him.

"You guys must be crazy."

The sergeant of the guard pushed and shoved his way through the soldiers to see what was the matter. The sergeant came forward and stood over Gordon. As Gordon looked up though blurred vision, he saw a robust square jaw line on a menacing face.

"What do we have here?" The sergeant asked.

"He's wearing the uniform of a union artilleryman, but he doesn't know the countersign, sergeant."

"Get him to his feet."

Two soldiers grabbed Gordon by the arms and yanked him up. His lip was bleeding from the rifle butt and his legs were wavering; he was faced with what appeared to be a monster. Gordon grimaced after smelling his breath of alcohol and chewing tobacco.

"Who might you be, boy?" The sergeant asked. He was impatient and even a little hostile toward him.

Gordon tried to shake from the grip of the guards. The sergeant motioned for his release. The guards let go.

"Gordon Smart."

"I don't know you. No one here seems to know you. And you don't know the countersign. Why's that?" The sergeant questioned.

"I don't know you people either!" Gordon said with contempt. He was forthright with his body language and the sergeant's anger elevated to the next level, but it didn't show other then a twitch to his right eye and one small drop of sweat running down his forehead. Other than that, he looked at Gordon very calmly and continued, "Do you know an Ernie Smith?"

Gordon thought for a moment; it seemed to be a harmless question. "No, I don't!"

The sergeant's piercing black eyes narrowed as he stared at Gordon. The right eye twitched again and that one bead of sweat continued to roll down his forehead to his cheek.

The sweat droplet fell from his face and landed with a splash on the ground in front of Gordon. At that instant, Gordon looked up and met the sergeant's fist hitting his nose, drawing blood. The sergeant drew his pistol from its holster and slapped Gordon hard across the left side of his face. The pistol's barrel ripped part of his earlobe and tore his cheek. Stunned, Gordon staggered back against the other soldiers and blood ran down his face.

The sergeant stared coldly back at Gordon and said, "You know him now!"

Gordon tried to control his bleeding with his hand. "You're crazy!"

"See that, you do know me!" The sergeant laughed a big belly laugh.

Gordon straightened and stared at the man who had just assaulted him. He studied his face. When paybacks were due, he didn't want to forget this guy.

When the sergeant stopped laughing, he looked over at the corporal and said, "Now take this rebel spy to the provost marshal. He can deal with him."

The corporal and another soldier roughly grabbed Gordon by the arms. "Let's go."

"Get off me! Take you're hands off me! Gordon yelled as he resisted.

The soldiers gained control of him and started toward the street.

"You're mad, all of you are mad." Gordon cried as they dragged him away with two more soldiers following close behind. Gordon was hauled a short distance. Then the corporal dropped him to the dirt road. "You're gonna walk or we're gonna kill you, right here, right now."

Gordon had no choice; he had to go along with them. Besides, he thought, *when I get there I'll report this to the event sponsor and call the police.*

They walked up Emmitsburg Road for a short distance, then turned right onto a foot path that went up and over Cemetery Ridge. They walked to another dirt road and followed it toward town. Their lanterns lit the way. Gordon couldn't see that well, but he saw a road sign that read Taneytown Road. The road was dirt; last time Gordon was there it was paved. What disturbed him more was the fact that there were no cars or trucks around. No late night factory noises. Then there was the stench of the soldiers. They smelled as if they hadn't seen a bath for a month.

They got to a two-story white farm house with a small front porch and an overhang roof.

The soldiers led Gordon into the front parlor where a large heavy set man sat behind an oak desk. He was the provost marshal. He was engrossed in paperwork and talked to himself while eating tomatoes. The corporal holding Gordon walked him across the dimly-lit room and handed him over to four other guards standing next to the desk where the provost marshal sat.

"Sir, this man tried to cross the picket line without the countersign, so we took him prisoner," The corporal said.

The marshal didn't look up from his work. He seemed too busy to deal with this interruption.

The corporal told the guards standing next to his desk, "He's all yours." He turned and sulkily saluted the marshal who still didn't look up from his desk.

The indignant corporal ordered an about face." Then he and marched his guard from the house.

The provost marshal, without showing emotion, stopped what he was doing. "Preparing tomorrow's passes for the civilians. Have a seat," the marshal ordered and went back to writing by the light of an oil lamp.

Gordon sat down in a chair next to his desk. He stared at the huge man with major shoulder straps. Gordon sat there waiting; his eye was swollen, and his face bleeding. He held his nose with his fingers trying to stop it from bleeding.

"Who are you?" the marshal asked.

"I want to call the police," Gordon requested.

Displaying a despotic attitude the marshal said, "I'm the police here."

"Those men assaulted me. I want them arrested. And I want you to call me an ambulance," Gordon insisted pointing at his bleeding head and face.

"You are in no position to have anyone arrested."

"Then I want to arrest you, too," Gordon said stomping his foot.

"What?" The major said.

"This tactical has gone too far," Gordon yelled and stood up.

"Sit down and empty your pockets. Place all your belongings on the table."

Gordon noticed the guard was on alert.

"Your full name?" the marshal asked ignoring his insubordination.

Gordon begrudgingly sat back down and gave him his name. "Gordon Mortimer Smart."

"What is that around you're neck?"

"Our commemorative metal that you people gave us."

"Place it on the table."

Gordon placed it on the table. "Here I don't want it anymore, I quit."

Without missing a step the marshal asked, "You can't quit. Unit and rank?"

"I said I *quit*."

"Quit? There's no quitting - unit and rank?"

"Private with Cushing's Battery. Where is this all going?"

"Cushing's Battery? He picked up his journal and ran his finger down the page to find what units were brought up to the front. "You must mean Battery A, Fourth U.S. Artillery?"

Gordon nodded his head.

"When did they name the battery after the lieutenant?"

"They named the battery after the lieutenant's death at the Angle."

"His death! At what angle?"

"He died firing his gun while holding in his guts. Remember your history for Christ sake." Gordon was now very much annoyed with his ignorance.

"Well, Mister Gordon Mortimer Smart, for your information, the lieutenant, nor anyone else for that matter, can be dead as you say, because we've not had a battle where his battery is located." The marshal smugly eased back into his chair, rich with satisfaction. Then he jumped straight up from his chair. "Is it your mission to kill Lieutenant Cushing?"

"No, of course not," Gordon said.

The marshal now showed suspicion. "You're a spy out to infiltrate our lines. Confess, and I will let you live. Lie and I'll see that you have a date with the hangman."

Gordon felt threatened. "You are as mad as everyone else."

"Yes, everyone's mad but you. Come on, I'm waiting, what do you have to say for yourself?"

"Unbelievable," Gordon muttered.

"You're unbelievable. Never mind, never mind, its late, we'll talk in the morning at a godlier hour for civilized men. I will inform Captain Hazard about you. We'll get to the bottom of this."

The marshal wrote Gordon's infractions down in his ledger. He then opened the top desk drawer and pulled out a small box. He slid Gordon's stuff into the box and closed the drawer. "Place him in the basement." He told the guard.

"Basement? Are you crazy? What the hell is going on here? I never have been to a reenactment where everyone stayed in character like this." Gordon thought a moment. "You're hazing me. You can't haze people. It's against the law."

The major looked sternly into Gordon's eyes. He spoke in an obnoxious authoritative tone. "If anyone's crazy, it's you. Guards, get him out of here." The major eased back in his chair and relaxed.

The guards grabbed him by the arms and led him down a set of steps to the basement. They gave him a blanket and pushed him down the remainder of the steps.

"I have rights, you know," he shouted up the steps.

Gordon found himself in a dark, musty-smelling room with a dirt floor. He felt around the walls trying to find a way out. The room seemed to be about ten feet by twelve feet. The walls were damp and he didn't like feeling the slime.

He was all alone with only his thoughts and pain. He tried to get comfortable on the dirt floor with just the blanket the guard had given him. He folded it in half and placed it on the ground. He laid on his side, but the dirt floor smelled badly, like mildew. He rolled onto his back, but the dirt floor was too hard to stay that way. Plus, on his back, the blood in his nose ran into his throat. It seemed, no matter how he laid, he could not get comfortable, so he just laid there getting cold and hungry.

Lying there at the bottom of the steps, he tilted his head backwards peering up the steps and accented the last word of each sentence so that the man upstairs would hear him.

"In the morning, I'm going to tell Mike about this *shit!* We'll kick all your *asses!* Then after the *carnage*, maybe, just maybe, I'll call the *police!* They can have what's left of your sorry *asses!* Then we'll see who's the real *badass!*"

Chapter Eight

Thursday, July 2, 1863 - 4:30 A.M.

Mike and Ray were cramped under the lean-to, causing Mike to become restless. The air was clammy. The ground was hard and damp. Mike tossed and turned trying to get comfortable. His movements were limited by Ray, lying so close. This went on for most of the night.

Mike fell into a dream state, his mind raced through the events in the barn, then to these guys now holding them captive. He struggled in his sleep.

Mike's mind awoke, but his eyes weren't ready to open yet. He thought he heard the sound of cracks and pops, like firecrackers, in the distance. He rolled on his back. It was stiff from the hard ground. After a few moments, he heard thunder. He opened his left eye and tried to listen. The world seemed distant in his mind. He was not certain if he was still dreaming.

The next thing Mike heard was the captain yelling. "Skirmishers, first platoon, take intervals, double quick - MARCH!"

Mike watched as men ran past them. "Why so early?"

The clanking sound of gear was heard. A sense of urgency was in the air.

"Fall-in, let's go," the sergeant yelled as he ran past.

Mike tried to pull himself up, but his body was like dead weight. Mike crawled out from under the lean-to and looked around. The grass was wet from the morning dew. He kicked Ray's feet, "Get up, Ray, and check this out."

It was early morning, before sunrise, but the sky was light, revealing men in the field ahead.

Mike listened again to the thunder, this time more clearly. Something seemed wrong. He realized that it was not the sound of thunder, but cannon fire.

Mike closed his eyes trying to imagine what was going on. "Ray, get out here quick!"

Ray shot up like a wild man, hitting his head on the pole. "What the hell?" Ray said, rubbing his head. "Did we miss breakfast?"

Ray brought down the lean-to getting out. Men were running past them, forming up the company of skirmishers.

The camp seemed to be in complete chaos. Mike saw them running up and over the ridge.

"Come on, Ray, let's get while the gettin's good," Mike shouted over the noise.

"I haven't had my first cup of coffee yet," Ray said, confused.

The musket fire grew louder and seemed to be coming from the left, filling the valley with the smoke of black powder.

Mike ran to catch up with the frantic soldiers at the ridge. Then he peeled off to the right and went into the woods. He and Ray came out of the woods and found that they were on top of a hill. A mass of Union men were pointing their muskets right at them.

"Fire!" was ordered by an officer in blue. Bullets whizzed by Mike's head hitting trees next to him. "Jesus Christ, their using real ammo." The men in blue loaded and were about to fire again.

"RUN!" Mike yelled. He changed direction and went back down the slope. He saw men in butternut and gray moving into a wooded area.

"This way, Ray," Mike yelled. They ran down the ridge and into the woods. They made it to the edge of a little creek with a gentle ascent on either side. Mike took a moment, he thought that he could take a shortcut to Route 116. "This way," he said and crossed the stream. The crackling of musket fire filled the woods.

They moved down into the smoke-filled wooded valley. Mike thought Ray was right behind him. The smoke and haze was so heavy, it made visibility poor.

Mike came up on the tail end of a company running just ahead. He was on their heels when a large explosion knocked him to the ground.

Mike lay still for a while, grabbing his ears as a deafening ring went through his head. He opened his eyes to the horror of body parts literally blown apart right in front of him.

"They're mad," Mike said as he looked around for Ray. "Where's Ray?" Mike desperately searched through the thick smoke, but he couldn't make out a thing in the woods. Nothing was making any sense. He looked to his right and saw the large crater left by a cannonball.

A figure emerged from the gray ash cloud and shouted something, but Mike couldn't make out what it said. The painful ringing in his ears made it hard to hear. He stood, staring in confusion. Distress numbed his body. A soldier in gray grabbed Mike's arm and hoisted him along. Everything became surreal as the two ran forward through the woods.

Another large blast landed near them. Mike could feel the man's grip tighten. Still in shock, Mike noticed that the man's hand was sill clenching his arm, but there was no man now: only his arm. Mike pulled the disembodied arm from himself and threw it on the ground.

Mike's immediate thought now was for Ray's safety and his own survival. He wanted to get out of the woods and fast. *Where the hell did he go?* Mike's mind went in circles as soldiers in gray rushed passed him. They seemed like ghosts in a fog, sweeping down into the valley.

He searched for Ray but saw only the dead bodies of men hunched over tree stumps. Some were missing limbs while others were still twitching with the last spasms of life as their death rattles faded away.

Figures appeared and disappeared through the smoke and trees as if running in and out of existence. Mike looked at the gruesome scene strewn with bodies of the dead and dying.

Mike stumbled to a little creek and crossed it. Through the trees, he saw the gray masses of the rebel infantry deploying within its fields.

Mike started in that direction, but two men ran past him, almost knocking him down. Then he saw several figures charging straight at him with fixed bayonets. Mike felt that this was the end, that he would be killed, his body left to rot in these miserable woods. But, to his relief, the men separated and ran around him. They were rebels in hot pursuit of the two Union men. Mike had forgotten to look at what color they were. He even forgot what color he was.

Another Confederate coming from the same direction grabbed Mike's arm and pulled him in the other direction, deeper into the woods. "Come on we got 'em on the run."

Mike pulled his arm from his grip, but everything was happening so fast he had no time to think. He ran after the man. The ringing in his ears penetrated his mind. He felt as if he would go crazy. They crossed the stream and started up the hill. The man continued up and over the ridge, but Mike stopped. He noticed something in a puddle of blood and guts. Something shiny caught his eye within the yellowish-gray intestines of what was a human being.

He knelt down and shoved his hand into the slimy pile of flesh and fished out a silver flip-top Zippo lighter.

Mike was filled with overwhelming fear and dread. "Ray!" he tried to yell, but couldn't. No one was there that could help anyway. All hope seemed lost. The nightmare had taken over. Mike felt his heart bursting in his chest as he knelt in the dirt, cradling his friend's lighter.

Chapter Nine

Thursday, July 2, 1863 - 4:49 A.M.

Lying there on the moist dirt floor of the basement, Gordon thought he heard a rooster crow. He opened his eyes and sat up to listen. He could hear movement outside, wagons rumbling, men shouting, and the hoof beats of the horses. He heard the muffled sound of cannon fire through the walls. "That's just great. Start without me," Gordon grumbled.

The basement of the small farmhouse was dark. There were no windows. After a few hours the walls had begun to close in on Gordon, making it feel like a tomb. It had been a rough night, but finally, in spite of his anger and pain, he had gotten a few hours sleep. The bleeding had stopped and he patted his face with the blanket in an attempt to clean it.

Sitting there with only his thoughts, Gordon was disappointed with how things had turned out. He put his face in his hands and mumbled, "Why are they acting this way?"

He was supposed to be enjoying a nice weekend camping with friends, having breakfast over a campfire using tin plates and cups. Now that everything had gone wrong, he really missed Mike and Ray.

The cellar door opened and Gordon heard the sound of brogans coming down the steps. Two guards appeared in front of him. "The provost marshal will see you now."

With the morning blur still clouding his thoughts Gordon rubbed his eyes and slowly got up.

The guards held out heavy iron handcuffs. They were the old kind: shackles, with a hinge that swung open. Gordon placed his hands in them and the hinge swung back into place. The guards locked them with a large key.

They also placed leg shackles on his ankles.

"Still playing games, while I miss everything," Gordon said. Now, on top of everything else, he worried about what waited for him at the top of the steps.

The guards motioned him to come with them. In disbelief, Gordon followed them up the steps to the front parlor the leg shackles dragging and clanging with each step.

Standing there before him was a captain and a lieutenant. They looked authentic in their weathered uniforms. Gordon noticed their attention to detail in the design the room. No modern furnishings. All the props were of the proper year.

The provost marshal, sitting behind his oak desk, shifted in his seat. Eyeing Gordon in the shackles, he made the introductions. "Captain Hazard, Lieutenant Cushing, this is Gordon Smart.

"I'm Captain Hazard of the 4th U.S. Artillery. Major Howard here says you have information to share with us?"

Gordon stood in silence. He didn't quite know what to say. This guy looked exactly like the dapper gentleman Captain Hazard from Civil War photos. But what had happened to John Cullom who was supposed to play him this weekend?

He looked around the room. There was a large man in the shadowed corner of the room. Gordon looked, but could not see. *Who the hell is that?*

"I hear you can see the future," Hazard said breaking the silence.

"For the hundredth time, I'm here with my two friends Michael Hill and Raymond Hensley. We're here to reenact the battle of Gettysburg. It's just a game for Christ sake."

"A game? You're putting me in a predicament. No one here seems to know who you are, and the marshal told us you had some crazy story about the lieutenant here getting killed. What do you know about that?" Captain Hazard asked.

Gordon thought, *Why are they continuing this facade, this masquerade?* "Do you believe you can do this to me with absolutely no negative ramifications? Without being arrested? Have you all lost you're minds? I'll sue all you're asses."

"I think you underestimate the position you are in. Do you realize that you are being held as a spy while in the service of the Confederate Army, which is an act of treason against the United States and thus punishable by death?" Captain Hazard asked.

Gordon stood in silence. The words echoed in his mind.

"This is not a game, Mister Smart. This is war, and war criminals will be dealt with," Captain Hazard said.

Provost Marshal Major Howard rose from his seat. "We'll get it out of you one way or the other; you will break." He motioned with his hand to the man standing in the shadows. "He should be able to persuade you."

The man stepped out from the shadows. He was dressed in a faded blue uniform with his hat brim angled up.

"Jesus, he looks like Jaws from the James Bond movies." Gordon recognized him instantly and almost fainted. Sergeant Earnest Smith.

Aghast, all Gordon wanted to do now was go to his happy place. The sergeant walked over to Gordon, stood in front of him, stared with hollow black eyes and said, "Hello. Remember me?"

The sergeant told the guards to take him into the bedroom. As the guards walked Gordon into the room the sergeant followed and shut the door.

***

The sergeant put on a pair of leather gloves that fit tight on his hands. He walked up to Gordon and punched him in the stomach. Gordon let out a groan and went to the floor in excruciating pain.

"Come on, boy, you can do better than that. This is just the beginning." The sergeant had to pick Gordon up, and then punched him in the mouth. Gordon's lip opened up again and started bleeding, but he was still standing.

Seeing this, Smith punched him in the stomach again. Gordon went to his knees. Smith bent over him and said, "We having fun yet?"

***

Major Howard sat behind his desk listening to the cries of the prisoner as he was beaten in the other room. After about ten minutes, Captain Hazard had had enough. "Okay, let's see if he's ready to talk before Smith kills him." Major Howard agreed. Gordon lay on the floor, a bloody mess, barely able to open his eyes. The major squatted beside him. "You ready to start talking some sense?"

Gordon had recoiled deep into his mind and did not respond. The major pulled him by his hair. "Do you hear me, boy?"

Gordon just laid there bleeding. Major Howard stood up and motioned for Smith to start again.

Smith kicked Gordon in the ribs and then grabbed his hair. "We can keep this up all day and all night if you want."

With blood dripping from his mouth Gordon finally mustered up the strength to cough out, "Okay, what do you want to know?"

"Everything," Sergeant Smith said.

"I know history - is that what you want?"

The sergeant bent over closer to Gordon's ear. "Tell me your mission. Look, you know I can't let you go, but I promise you this: if you cooperate, I will make this hurt less."

"Please, I can give you the Confederate positions if that's what you want. Just don't hurt me anymore."

The sergeant stopped. "He's broke, Major. He'll tell you anything you want to know."

Major Howard's eyes lit up and he motioned for Gordon's torturer to leave. "Thank you, Sergeant, you are excused now."

The sergeant stood up and walked out of the room.

"Go on," Major Howard said.

"Let me think... what's today's date?" Gordon managed.

"What does that matter?" Howard asked.

"Please," begged Gordon, "I need to know so that I can tell you where they'll be."

"July second," snapped Howard.

"And the year?" Gordon asked checking to see how confused he might be.

Major Howard's face became red with anger. "I've had just about enough of your nonsense. If you don't get to the point and get to it fast - God help me— I'll kill you myself." He drew a blade from his belt and held it to Gordon's throat.

"Okay, let's say this is July second. Little Round Top will be attacked in the afternoon."

"Guard, get a pencil and paper," Howard said pressing the knife harder against Gordon's throat. "What the hell is Little Round Top?"

"The mountain to the south," Gordon squeaked out.

Howard took a piece of paper and placed it in front of him. He gave Gordon a pencil. "I want you to write down everything."

"What is your mission here exactly?" Captain Hazard interrupted.

"It's in all the history books," Gordon said.

Captain Hazard straightened. He seemed to be reading Gordon's body language, evaluating whether he was lying or not.

"He's crazy, just like I said. He can wait in the basement for his court martial," Major Howard announced.

"Court martial! Wait, I can prove I'm telling the truth," Gordon said quickly.

"How's that?" Captain Hazard asked.

"I have the history book in my knapsack. You can read it for yourself."

"Where's your knapsack?" Captain Hazard asked.

"It's outside in my tent."

Captain Hazard whispered something in Lieutenant Cushing's ear. The lieutenant then went to the door and told one of the guards.

"What else do you know?" Captain Hazard continued.

"The Wheat Field and the Peach Orchard will also be attacked today."

"That's vague, don't you think? What peach field? Which wheat field?" Major Howard asked with a skeptical look to his face.

"I can draw you a map of their locations, plans, movements, all of it. I not only read the book, I studied it."

"Okay, but I do have one more question." Captain Hazard said.

"What?" Gordon asked guarded.

"Do we win?" Captain Hazard asked, on a whim.

"As a matter of fact, we do," Gordon said.

Hazard looked unconvinced.

Then Lieutenant Cushing asked. "Why were you sent to kill me of all people?"

"I wasn't sent -"

Just then the door opened and the guard brought in a young dapper man in his early twenties. Gordon sized up the man who wore long dark sideburns.

"Who's this?" Major Howard asked the guard.

"Private Mortimer Smart sir, he's the only Smart out there. We searched through his things. There was no such book, sir."

Gordon was shocked. Was this supposed to be his great-great-grandfather? The only picture Gordon had of Mortimer was one taken after the war when he was a much older man. However, he always heard that his great-great-grandfather was a sergeant major, not a private.

"Private Smart, do you know this man?" Howard asked.

Mortimer looked closely at Gordon and was appalled to see his condition: Gordon was covered in blood.

"No... can't rightly say, but I do have a right size family, sir."

"There is no history book, is there? You are just a spy and a bad one at that." Captain Hazard told Gordon. He was visibly disappointed.

"My thought exactly," said the major, "he's a quack, crazy as a June bug. Private Smart, you're dismissed."

The screen door slapped the wooden jamb when the young man left. Major Howard, now beyond upset sternly said, "I'll order a court martial for this afternoon and we can hang him tomorrow."

Captain Hazard agreed. "Let's get back to the war."

"I'll send a report up the lines to General Hancock," Howard said.

"Hang me! What? Who the hell are you people?" Gordon was in a frenzy. After hearing those words his mind raced for something else to say but instead, out of instinct, he lunged forward with all of his remaining strength and made a dash for the front door. His legs, still shackled, restricted his stride, but he made it to the door.

The club that struck his face sent him crashing back to the wooden deck. Standing over him was Sergeant Earnest Smith. He dragged Gordon back into the parlor.

"Put this traitor back in the basement, and leave him in the shackles," Major Howard ordered.

The guards dragged him to the foot of the steps and rolled him down into the basement.

Captain Hazard picked up his gloves from the table and started out the door. Lieutenant Cushing quickly opened the door for the captain and held it until he passed.

At the bottom of the steps, Gordon's eyes began to dim, and he faded into unconsciousness.

Chapter Ten

Pitzer's Woods - 8:30 A.M.

Kneeling on the ground in the woods, Mike wondered what the hell had just happened. He forced himself up from the ground after the encouragement of a passing Confederate. At least he had looked like a rebel wearing butternut; the dirt and bloodstains made it hard to tell.

"Where the hell am I?" Mike said aloud, trying to orient himself. A couple more men went by and he thought he'd follow them. *Maybe Route 116 is this way?*

He needed to get out of the woods and get his head together, to come to grips with what happened to Ray. Somehow, he had to make sense of it before calling the police.

As he walked along, Mike felt his head. There was blood from an open gash along his brow. He looked down at the lighter in his hand. "What will I tell Ray's mother, my God, his mom?" he whispered.

Mike began to think about his childhood with Ray. Growing up with Ray was a challenge, but had been fun. He always had to keep the bullies from beating the living crap out of him in high school. With Ray's big mouth, Mike learned to fight out of necessity.

Mike stopped, overcome with emotion. *I can't believe he's dead.* He felt responsible since he was the one who had talked him into coming in the first place. Mike saw soldiers walking toward a clearing.

He walked in their direction. He reached the edge of the woods and saw a large camp. *Is that the reenactment area?*

Suddenly, he felt a presence behind him. He looked over his shoulder, back into the woods. There she was, the woman in white, just standing there. She really was a vision of beauty. She waved for him to come nearer and then she spoke softly, "Follow the path, Michael."

"What path?" He yelled.

Mike looked around, *had anyone else seen or heard her? Apparently not.*

Astonished that she said his name, Mike felt a strange comfort. He was determined to talk to her. As he approached her, she went into the woods. "Who are you? How do you know me?" he called, but she kept moving, ghostlike, through the trees.

Mike ran after her, but she moved with ease between the trees until she disappeared. He searched for her, but couldn't see where she went. *What do you want from me?*

He walked in the same direction that he had last seen her. He looked down and there was a path. *Is this the path she's talking about?*

Mike followed it and spent the entire day wandering in the woods. He had to find her. He sensed that when he did, he would get some answers to this madness.

Mike heard cannon fire. Then the crackling of musket fire in the distance. Mike wanted to get out of the woods before dark. He knew in the dark, everything was different. *I don't want to spend the night in the woods,* he thought. *She said follow the path, and since the shooting is that way, I'll go this way.*

Mike followed the obscure trail into the tall brush down to a stream where the path stopped.

Mike noticed the sun. It was setting on his right as he followed the stream. *Must be walking south,* he thought. The woods got darker. The trees got higher. The shadows got longer as the orange ball got lower.

Mike was thirsty and getting hungry, so he walked down to the stream to get a drink. *Maybe I'll catch dinner.* As he got to the edge of the water, he suddenly heard the sounds of hoof beats. He listened. *Horses!*

He quickly hid in the thicket and got low as he could. It was a patrol coming his way at a fast pace. As the horses neared, they seemed to slow down. Mike saw that they were dressed in butternut. *Confederate cavalry; what are they looking for?*

Mike laid flat on the ground until the patrol moved on. He pushed off the ground with his hands to have a look. They were gone. *Good time to cross the stream. If this is Willoughby Run, and the sun sets in the west, then that way must be home.*

After fording the stream, Mike knew that he had left the path. He meandered along the stream, hoping she would reappear and show him the way. Then Mike heard voices. He got down and crawled toward the conversation. A small campfire glowed in a clearing up ahead. On his knees, he moved slowly closer so that he could get a better look.

He spotted four ragged soldiers sitting around a low campfire. They looked more like hobos in their tattered brown and butternut uniforms. There were two cavalrymen and two infantrymen.

The two infantrymen were having a conversation while the two cavalrymen cooked a meal.

They may be just as mad as the rest, he thought and decided to avoid them. He started to go around to the right when one of the cavalrymen saw him and jumped up with his guns drawn. He alarmed the others and they all jumped up garnishing their revolvers.

"You there - whatta-ya want?" a long-haired, wild-eyed man asked.

Mike showed them that he was unarmed. "I mean you no harm. I'm hungry and I'm tried and I don't want any trouble."

"Shoulda thought of that before you come sneaking into our camp. How me'n mah boys know'd you're not the law?" The wild eyed man said.

"First off, I wasn't sneaking into you're camp. Second, I have no gun. Would a lawman come into you're camp unarmed?" Mike said.

"He gotta point there, Jake," said the other cavalryman standing next to the wild-eyed man.

"Point, my ass," Jake said as he spit his black chew on the ground. "You a deserter, mebbe?"

"Just trying to go home," Mike replied.

"So's we," said the infantryman.

"Can he stay, Jake?" asked the other infantryman.

"Givin' the situation," Jake said, and then cautiously put his gun away and sat back down.

They all lowered their guns and took their seats around the campfire. Watching the glowing embers and the smoke eddy up in spirals, the four began to relax with their new guest.

"So, what unit you with?" asked the nicer cavalryman.

"Ninth Virginia -"

"What is this, old home week? You said you were hungry, so what did you bring us to eat?" Jake asked.

"I don't have any food."

"Goddamn it, Earl, he's not eatin' mine" Jake said getting contentious.

Jake was a hard-looking man with long, dirty blond hair. He seemed to be the meanest of the bunch.

Mike looked at what was cooking over the fire. Earl was cooking up four rats on his ramrod, which he had rigged as a skewer.

"Ever eat rat?" Earl asked.

"No, I can't say that I have," Mike said.

"I know at least five recipes for cookin' up rats," Earl said with a grin as he turned the ramrod. With his fingers he added a little salt and pepper to spice them up.

When he was satisfied that they were done, the four men each had a rat to eat; Mike only could watch. The infantryman pulled off a piece of meat and handed it to Mike. "Here, have some of mine."

"Thanks," Mike said.

"Name's Lonny, yours?"

"Mike."

Jake looked at Mike and shook his head. "Listen asshole, next time, bring your own food."

Mike's blood started to boil, and his first thought was: *Who does this* Hill's Got Eyes *freak think he's talking to?* But he controlled himself and let the remark pass. He was eating, and that was all that mattered at the moment.

Mike cracked a smile and said, "Very tasty, complements to the chef."

Jake glared at Mike while Earl smiled. "What are you grinning at?" Jake asked Earl. "Not every day I get a complement on my cooking," Earl said.

"For Christ sakes," Jake said.

"Come on Jake, don't be so ornery," Earl said.

"I'm George by the way," said the infantryman sitting next to Lonny. He strangely blinked his eyes after each sentence.

"Nice to meet ya," Mike said.

After sucking on the bones of the rat, Lonny finally spoke up. "I just wanted to go home, too. I thought that I had the right to do so. I enlisted for twelve months and completed my volunteer obligations. Now they say I can't go home because of some new Conscript Act passed by the Confederate Congress which says they could hold me until the war is over."

Earl agreed. "Nevuh thought the gov'ment had the right to hold ya beyond your volunteer date."

"Because they're the gov'ment, that's why." Jake answered angrily. "I don't give a shit about obligations and I don't give a rat's ass about the army. I have one ambition now, and that's to get out, any way possible," Jake told them.

"I hate marching. There should be a law against it." George said.

Lonny, sitting next to George, laughed. "You just got to love 'em. Most don't see the beauty in so simple a thought. The army, with their sense of duty, sent him to company Q."

"What's company Q?" Mike asked.

"That's where they dispose of the stragglers or play-outs. They put George there because he's a little slow in the head." Lonny leaned toward Mike and whispered. "I tell you right now, it's safer in the regular company than with God only knows what kind of criminals. Besides, the army puts company Q up front of every battle to get rid of them," Lonny shuddered at the thought.

"Oh yeah, I did read something about that," Mike said.

"Read? You can read. I knew I didn't like you, I suppose you can add and subtract too," Jake said.

"Yeah, that too," Mike said. "So, how did two cavalrymen join up with two infantrymen?" Mike asked.

"We ran in to 'em in these here woods," Earl explained.

"These woods are bigger then I thought," Mike said.

Jake glared back at Mike. "You look familiar; do I know you from somewhere?"

"I don't believe so," Mike said. "How did you and Jake hook up?" Mike asked Earl.

"Hook up, what do we look like, a train?" Jake snickered.

Mike glared at Jake like he was an idiot.

Jake stared at Mike like he was a buffoon.

Earl interrupted the stare-down. "Me and Jake know'd each other a long time. I remembered a game me and a girl played right here in Gettysburg," Earl started. "Her mother had a box that she kept in a barn. Sarah, remember her Jake?" Earl glanced over at Jake. "She called it the tinderbox, remember, Jake?"

"Hold it right there, don't say another word to this nosy bastard," Jake said angrily.

"Who's he gonna tell, Jake? Hell, never gave it a thought until the army got so miserable. When me and Jake met up again, we came up with the idea of using the box to leave the army," Earl asked.

"Shut up your mouth, you dumb bastard, told you once, won't be a second." Jake looked like he meant it.

"Okay, Jake, don't have to get like that," Earl said.

"How these two fit in?" Mike asked, ignoring Jake's temper.

"Met here in the woods -"

"I said shut that mouf, jabber jaw," Jake said sternly.

"You shut yours, I'm trying to have a conversation here," Mike sternly told Jake.

Jake pulled his gun and pointed at Mike.

"Okay, okay," Earl said. "Cool down, you two." He pulled from his coat pocket some whiskey in a flask. "Anyone like a sip?"

"That's more like it," Lonny said, relieved that the duel of words was over for now.

Mike let things calm down. He tried to comprehend what Earl was taking about. *Is it possible he's referring to the same barn with the tinderbox he explored?* Now he thought he recognized Jake. *Nah, no way, impossible.* Mike heard a noise and looked up.

Suddenly, a shot rang out from the darkness. Lonny was struck between the eyes and fell over. George screeched as he saw his friend fall. Mike checked him and saw the back of his head was missing.

Meanwhile, Jake and Earl were running through the woods, putting distance between them and whoever shot at them.

"He's dead, let's go," Mike said, as he looked at George.

Mike realized it must be the Confederate patrol. They must have heard their voices and seen the campfire. The nearby trees were hit by the lead. Mike ducked from the rifle fire and hit the ground. He looked up to see George jumping over a fallen tree. He was running to catch up with his friends deep into the woods. Mike started to follow, but was stopped by the cavalrymen.

Chapter Eleven

Thursday, July 2 - 2:03 P.M.
Gordon had been unconscious when the guards rolled him down the cellar steps. Still entombed in the basement, he laid there on the dirt floor. The heavy iron handcuffs were still on his wrist and the shackles on his legs.

With every breath, dust swirled around his mouth from the dirt. Suddenly, he awoke with pain in both hands; the cuffs were cutting into his flesh. He rolled over with the odor of mildew and blood in his nose. His whole body was in pain. He felt his jaw and it was swollen along with his eyes. There was dry blood on his face and in his hair.

He tried to get up, but his right side hurt.

"My rib. Some weekend this turned out to be," Gordon said as he rolled on his back. He wanted to get as far away from the bastards as he could.

Lying there in sodden misery, Gordon heard a scream from the outside. Then he heard what sounded like an explosion. He heard the rattling of wagons being drawn along uneven terrain. *Crazy,* he thought. *Nah, couldn't be.*

As if the pain to his body wasn't bad enough, hunger had begun to set in. Then he heard the heavy footsteps of brogans coming down the wooden steps again. It was the federal guard.

"Get up, spy. The provost marshal wants to see you," said the sergeant of the guard.

Life seemed to drain from Gordon's face. He felt a moment of panic, and had to resist the impulse to scream. *Calm down, maybe I can reason with them.*

The sergeant was running his fingers down his goatee waiting on Gordon to get up.

"Let's go," the sergeant said impatiently, and then grabbed Gordon and pulled him to his feet.

"Ouch." Gordon bent in pain.

The guard led him up the stairs to the open door by the sentry at the top of the steps. Gordon shielded his eyes from the light as he entered the front parlor. He was placed on an army bread box next to the provost marshal's desk. Gordon recognized him as Major Howard.

Gordon sat anxiously staring, waiting on what the marshal would say. As he looked around the room, Gordon saw the man who said he was Captain Hazard seated in a comfortable chair directly across from the marshal's desk. Beside him was a stern-looking, young first lieutenant.

Gordon didn't recognize the lieutenant sitting impatiently, tapping his foot on the wooden floor, waiting for the proceeding. The lieutenant had a rat-like face and a Groucho Marx mustache.

"Let's get started," Major Howard said. "Why do you feel the need to kill him, Lieutenant Akers?"

"We've been through this already, major. Can't you just tell the prisoner of our agreement?"

"I haven't been completely convinced yet," Major Howard said angrily.

"May I remind the provost marshal, that his crime is that of treason? He's a spy, and we are obligated to hang spies."

"Whoa, hold on just a minute," Gordon exclaimed. "Me -hang me - who do you think you are?" Gordon's first impression had been correct: rat face was a jerk.

"No one's hanging anyone, at least not yet," Captain Hazard said.

"His actions may have cost the lives of many men," Akers argued.

"Your passion is noted, Lieutenant Akers," Major Howard pointed out.

"I think we should spare this man's life for one reason, and one reason alone: his information," Captain Hazard snapped.

"His information is wrong. The enemy is swinging around to our left flank and taking the high ground. They're climbing the little rocky hill as we speak."

Captain Hazard seemed to get impatient. "Then we better get back to the war then."

"I say we simply take him outside and shoot him right now," Akers argued.

Gordon jumped up from the box he was sitting on.

"What is wrong with you people? We're all reenactors. You're not a major, no more then I'm a spy. As I said before, I'm here with Michael Hill and Raymond Hensley. I've had enough of this first person crap, it's only a reenactment." Gordon got up and ran to a window, "Look, damn it, does that look like a real battle?"

As Gordon looked through the glass he saw a mass of men, horses, and wagons on the move. And then one of the wagons exploded. The horses killed, the men on the wagon were torn apart. He felt the blood drain from his face. "Where am I?" He stood there with a blank look on his face.

Two guards grabbed him and forced him back down on the wooden cracker box and held him there. Gordon sat with his head hung low. He didn't know what to make of the visions he had just seen. "How did you do that?" he skeptically asked.

"Do what?" Akers asked.

"I'm being filmed, aren't I? America's Funniest Home Videos or Candid Camera, right?" Gordon looked around the room for the cameras.

"What is wrong with him?" Akers said.

"Melancholy," Captain Hazard said.

"That's no excuse. They shoot mad dogs, don't they?" Akers said.

Captain Hazard frowned, "I still don't like the idea of losing information."

"I understand your position, Captain Hazard, but there is the question of the integrity of this court. Discipline must be observed," Major Howard advised.

"At the very least, we can hang him after the battle?" Captain Hazard offered, in hope of keeping any valuable information long enough to win the battle.

"Agreed," Lieutenant Akers quickly injected.

Gordon was in complete disbelief. "I know the law, you can't try me in absentia," he yelled.

"I don't know where the hell absentia is, but I find you guilty as charged here," Major Howard said.

Frightened, Gordon stared at the floor. "You got me okay, I'm scared, now stop it. I've had enough."

"The war, gentlemen," Captain Hazard prompted the marshal.

Major Howard hurried under pressure. "You sir, are a spy, therefore, as provost marshal, I sentence you to death by hanging. A firing squad is too good for the likes of you. The sentence to be carried out, as soon as the war will allow."

Suddenly, the door swung open and in came the aide-de-camp. "Good news, gentlemen."

"What is it?" Major Howard snapped.

"Little Round Top was saved. The Twentieth Maine held the hill."

"What the hell is Little Round Top?" Major Howard asked.

"The little rocky hill to the south, sir," the aide explained.

"Oh yes, that hill," the marshal said remembering what Gordon had said earlier.

"How did they do that?" Captain Hazard asked.

"Colonel Chamberlain charged down the hill with fixed bayonets and pushed the Rebs back down the line."

"So, his information isn't so flawed after all, now is it, lieutenant?" Captain Hazard said looking over at Akers.

Lieutenant Akers stood in disbelief. Major Howard motioned to remove Gordon from the room. The guards then grabbed Gordon by the arms and started to escort him toward the basement.

"But wait, I can help," Gordon finally managed to say. He was trying to spare himself the basement. "I don't know how it happened, but I'm here, in the past."

"Sure you are, put him in the basement," Major Howard told the guards.

In a desperate attempt to keep his freedom, Gordon yelled, "Don't you understand, I know what's going to happen next."

A guard elbowed him in the bad rib and Gordon buckled over in pain. He was bodily led to the basement once again. This time they let him walk down the steps. Once he reached the basement floor, Gordon's demeanor changed from that of a beaten man to that of a determined man. He knew what he had to do. And he had to do it fast. Time wasn't on his side any longer. The only option now was escape.

Chapter Twelve

Pitzer Woods - 9:13 P.M.

Surrounded by the Confederate cavalry, Mike was staring down the barrel of a .44 caliber army pistol. He looked around, and there were six .52 caliber Sharps box-lock carbines all pointed his way.

"Don't you move," said the stocky-built sergeant upon his black charger.

"Don't worry, I'm not going anywhere," Mike answered. He looked around, wondering how the cavalry had come through the woods. Then he saw that they were on a bridle path.

"Where's the gold you stole from General Stuart's strongbox?" The sergeant said in a raspy voice.

"What gold?"

"Don't play dumb, boy. You know what gold."

"Look, I don't know anything about any gold. Those fellows you chased out of here probably took it."

"You're under arrest."

"Sure, but there is one problem," Mike said.

"What's that?" the sergeant asked.

"You're on horses - I'm on foot - and we're in a forest."

"So... can you outrun bullets?" The sergeant said.

"Let's see," Mike yelled directly in the face of the sergeant's horse and threw his hands up, spooking the animal. He then ran between the sergeant and another trooper, scaring his horse as well, and throwing the trooper off balance.

Two troopers got off shots as Mike ran into the woods. As the soldiers turned the horses in his direction, Mike zigzagged and ducked between trees.

"Look at that boy skedaddle. Guess he can outrun bullets," a trooper observed.

Mike ran harder then he had ever run before as shots chased after him. He didn't stop running until he was out of breath, and even then he walked another mile just to put distance between them.

Mike walked the dark woods looking for a way out. He still couldn't believe Ray was not with him. Mosquitoes pestered him as waited on the light from the moon to come out from behind a cloud, which would then allow him to see and go a little farther.

Then, in the distance, Mike saw a glow, seemingly in the middle of nowhere. He walked towards the light and found himself standing in front of an old house. A whitewashed, wooden picket fence outlined the border of the front lawn. The soft glow of light was coming from a window.

He swung open the gate and walked to the front porch steps. It was an old, two-story farm house in need of some repair. Cautiously, he walked up the porch steps and looked in the window.

Mike saw the same man from the campfire just hours before, Jake. He was pointing a gun at an attractive young woman who also seemed familiar. They seemed to be arguing. Mike pressed his face against the window trying to see her a little better. His heart sank to his stomach that had suddenly become full of butterflies. "It's her, the woman in white," he whispered.

He couldn't believe it. Out here, in the middle of nowhere, here she was. Then he saw Earl. "Where's the third?" Mike mumbled as he scanned the pallor. Then he spotted George. He was standing at the front door seemingly guarding it.

Then Mike heard Jake threaten the woman. "Hand it over or else."

"The tinderbox is dangerous, you hardheaded scalawag," she said.

"Hand it over," Jake said, raising the pistol to her head.

Mike became alarmed. "Shit, he's going to kill her," he said.

Mike ran to the front door. As he rushed in, he grabbed George and held him as a shield and hostage. Mike had George's gun pointed directly at his head. "Drop your gun, Jake."

"You first," said a voice from behind Mike. Earl had rounded a corner of the adjacent room and was pointing his gun at Mike.

"You might get one of us, but the other will get you," Jake said.

"Stop it, all of you," the woman in white yelled.

"Just hand over the tinderbox and we'll be on our way," Jake said.

"You do realize how dangerous it is? Earl, why did you bring that scalawag into this house? You don't want to use the tinderbox to escape, good Lord; it opens doors you don't want to enter. You could change the path of history."

"That's exactly why I'm here, don't ya see Sarah? That's the best way to escape. Maybe history needs changing," Jake said.

"Not by the likes of you," Sarah said.

"Enough talk. Shoot him, Earl," Jake ordered.

"What about George?" Earl asked.

"What about George?"

"Well, he's in the way," Earl pointed out.

George blinked a few times. His face looked for compassion from Jake.

"Ya dumb bastard, we don't need George," Jake said.

Earl took aim at Mike's head, George blinked uncontrollably. Then another familiar voice was heard: "Drop your weapons or I'll blow your brains out."

Mike looked over to see Ray holding a pistol.

Ray had come from the rear bedroom with a gun. For the second time tonight, Mike swallowed his heart. Here was the guy he had to save twice a day for the last twenty years, now saving his life.

Ray had brought the situation to a stalemate. Then Sarah walked between Mike and Jake.

"What are you doing?" Mike said, now worried that she might get hurt.

"Just go... the tinderbox is back at the barn. I don't want any killing in this house," Sarah warned.

"It's not there, we looked," Jake said.

"You didn't look hard enough," Sarah told him.

Jake stared hard at her. "Okay, I believe you," he said and let out his breath in a sigh of relief. Then he raised his gun and shot past Sarah and into George. George fell limp into Mike's arms. His eyes were wide open as he bled out. There was no blinking now. He was dead. Sarah screamed and ducked. Mike swung the body of George into Earl. Ray shot at Jake, making him jump for cover behind the sofa.

"Earl, you okay?" Jake asked.

"Yeah."

"Follow me," Jake said and got up shooting and ran for the window. Mike returned fire, but Jake jumped through the window onto the porch, unscathed. Broken glass went flying as Earl ran out the front door. Mike ran to the window only to see both of them run as fast as they could into the woods.

"Let's get 'em, Ray," Mike shouted.

Sarah stopped him, "Wait, and calm down."

"But they're getting away."

"Yes, I know, but you do have time," she said.

"But," Mike said impatiently.

She took Mike's hand. Her sweet and kind character calmed Mike. For some reason he knew he could trust her.

"Let's all go into the kitchen and calm down. I'll put on a pot of coffee. There's a lot to tell you." She let go of his hand and walked into the kitchen.

Mike, savoring her sweet smell of lavender, turned to Ray and gave him a big man-hug, and then he shoved Ray as if he were mad. "What the hell happened? Why ain't you dead?"

"Yeah, good to see you again, too, Mike."

"So where did you go?" Mike asked.

"That was some unbelievable bullshit today," Ray began, "real ammo, real killing; all hell broke loose. People were running everywhere. After I lost you, the fighting seemed to ease up a bit, giving me a moment to light a cigarette."

"Wait, you took a smoke break?" Mike was stunned.

"You say that like there's something wrong with it? I was trying to think."

"Go on, I want to hear this," Mike said with a smile.

"Suddenly, there was a huge blast and some asshole knocked me to the ground. When I went to get up, there were someone's guts all over me. What's worse, my cigarette was knocked out of my mouth and I lost my lighter. I looked all over for it and couldn't find it."

Mike reached into his pocket and brought out the Zippo. "Here," he said and handed it back to Ray.

Completely dumbfounded, Ray only said, "Thanks." He pulled a pack of cigarettes from his pocket and looked at them. "Hum, three left," then he lit one up. Mike stared and shook his head, "Unbelievable."

They went into the kitchen and had a seat at the table. Sarah started coffee, and then walked to the table and sat down beside Mike. The lovely smell of lavender filled Mike's senses as he looked into her light blue eyes.

"Here, let me clean your wound," She said softly.

"What wound?" Mike asked.

"The cut to your head. Let me start from the beginning."

"Let's start with, who are you?" Mike asked.

"Oh, sorry for my rudeness, I am Sarah. Introductions were always my weak point. Allow me to explain; I used to live in town with my parents. They were Pennsylvania Dutch and practiced Wicca. Earl and I were childhood neighbors and we used to play in my father's barn. One day Earl found a box that belonged to my mother under the floorboards of the hayloft."

"The tinderbox," Mike guessed, remembering what Earl said.

"Yes, the poem is a page from *The Book*. It has the power to open doors to the future or past."

"The book?" Mike asked.

"Some call it *The Long Lost Friend.*"

"How does..."

"It work? Don't know that for sure, but we played hide and seek with it not realizing how dangerous it really was."

"Wow," Mike said.

"That scoundrel Earl must have told Jake about it. He lived on the outskirts of town," then she whispered, "The other side of the tracks. After that, the whole town knew and it became a right size scandal."

Ray heard a low whistle and interrupted. "Coffee's ready."

Mike shot Ray a look. Sarah finished wrapping Mike's head, got up, and walked over to the pot on the stove. She poured them each a cup, and then sat back down next to Mike.

"What happened next?" Mike asked.

"It wasn't long before my parents were accused of being witches and we were run out of town. My father owned this place, so we moved here. They were good people, healers, they wouldn't harm anyone."

"I'm sorry, Sarah," Mike said.

"At the end of each month mother would take the buckboard into town to buy groceries. When the war started things went from bad to worse. On her last trip to town, she never came home. She was later found dead along the road. A month passed after father buried her and he saddled up and went into town to find out what the sheriff was doing about it. His body was found in an alley behind the blacksmith.

"That's incredible, I'm so sorry," Mike said.

"After my parents' death, I never gave the tinderbox a second thought. I didn't believe I had the healing power of my mother or father. But with the war, I became a nurse volunteer. That's when I started to realize I had the power, too.

"What do Jake and Earl want with the tinderbox?" Mike asked.

"Jake and Earl both wanted to escape the war. Jake did and ended up in your future. I telepathically sent my image there. I got into your mind when you touched Jake in the street."

"That's why I could see you but my friends couldn't," Mike said, beginning to understand.

"Yes. When your friend read the spell, you all came through the doorway and reset the events of time. We now have a second chance to stop Jake from using the box."

"So that's how we got here. What do you need me to do?" Mike asked.

"You must stop Jake. He is headed for the barn again. You must beat him at his own game. Get to the barn first and get the tinderbox."

"Is this the same red barn on Steinwehr Avenue?" Mike asked.

"That name is unfamiliar to me. The barn I'm talking about is located along Emittsburg Road," Sarah said.

Mike remembered that in 1863, the whole road into the town was called Emittsburg Road. In later years it was renamed after the Union general that protected the town. "Yes, I'm with you now," Mike said.

"Goodness graces, once you're in the barn, you can use the spell to get back home," Sarah said.

"There is one problem," Mike said.

"Problem, what problem?" Ray asked.

"The barn is now the front lines of the Union army."

Ray sank into his seat. Sweat began to form on his brow. "Shit, how the hell are we supposed to get to the barn, now?"

"What about Lee's final charge?" Mike asked.

"What charge?" Ray asked.

"Picket's Charge," Mike said.

"Oh, hell no!" Ray sank deeper into his seat, pondering the implications. "Mike, remember, our regiment, the Ninth Virginia. They had seventy five percent loses in that charge. They made it over the wall, you know, the Angle."

"That's why we joined that particular regiment," Mike remembered.

"Do you recall Pickett's response to General Lee's request to turn to his division? He said he had no division!"

Mike was stunned: Ray actually remembered the words. "Yeah, so what?"

"We stand a real good chance of being killed," Ray yelled.

"Calm down Ray," Mike said, "Maybe we don't have to make that charge."

As Mike pondered, Sarah interrupted. "You must find your third friend."

"You know about Gordy?" Mike asked.

"I saw three, two gray, one blue."

"I'll be damned," Mike said.

"The three of you must be in close proximity, and read the spell word for word."

"But didn't you say that the tinderbox was dangerous?" Ray asked.

"It can be."

Ray's mind was headed into la-la-land when Mike grabbed him by the arm. "I'll think of something."

"What about Gordy?" Ray asked.

"I'll figure it out."

Ray didn't like it, but he had no other options; he agreed with a nod of his head.

"If it would make you feel better, Ray, I will place a spell over the both of you," Sarah said. "You know, to keep you safe from harm."

"You can do that?" Ray asked.

"I am a witch, haven't you heard?"

"Somehow, that don't make me feel any better," Ray said.

Sarah picked up *The Book*, and then lit a white candle. She opened to the page that said, A Charm against Powder and Ball. As she read she waved her hand over the both of them making the sign of the cross. "May the Lord watch over you?" She was finished. "There, that ought to do it."

"Thank you, Sarah," Mike said.

"Well, Sarah, it's time to go," Mike said.

"Don't you need some rest?"

"Not while Jake and Earl is getting away. We already gave them a good head start."

Mike looked at the grandfather clock in the hallway. It read four o'clock. "That late already. Come on Ray, we better get going."

Mike was putting on his coat when Sarah came up to him and began to straighten out his coat. "Be sure to turn the hour glass over to start the timer. Read the words exactly as written."

"Okay, Sarah," Mike said. She handed him his hat.

"Here, I made up papers for you and Ray to get through the picket line."

"Papers?" Mike was confused. *When did she have time to do all this?*

"These papers say you are returning from a field hospital."

As he examined the papers, the next sensation Mike felt was Sarah's lips on his forehead along with the sweet scent of lavender tingling his olfactory nerves.

"Thank you for saving my life last night," she whispered.

"You're perfectly welcome," Mike said as his knees weakened. He leaned into her. She kissed him on the lips. Mike's brain began to fill with endorphins and adrenaline. But, he realized there was no time for this to continue.

He turned and walked over to Ray with a little more lift in his step. "How are you feeling, Ray?"

"Better," Ray answered staring back at what just happened between his best friend and the stranger, Sarah.

Sarah walked to Ray and checked his wounds from the explosion the day before. She seemed to be delighted with the healing.

"Think you can travel?" Mike asked Ray.

"I said so, didn't I?" Ray said, as he shouldered his haversack.

"Then let's go."

Mike and Ray walked down the front steps of the old house while Sarah stood in the doorway, watching. It was early morning and still dark. The moon, again, provided the light for their journey.

"Do take care of yourselves." Sarah said as she smiled and waved goodbye. Ray looked at Mike who had a big grin on his face. "What's up between you two?"

"I think I've been smitten," Mike said.

Ray shook his head in amusement as the two walked into the woods and disappeared.

Chapter Thirteen

July 2, 1863 - 8:03 P.M.
Gordon was pent-up again in the musty-smelling basement. After the kangaroo court, his mind was full of questions. *Time travel? Is that even possible? But how? Where's Mike and Ray? Are they here, too?*

The door at the top of the steps opened and the light shone down on him. The guard walked down the steps and placed a plate of beans on the floor along with a tin cup of water. "Here's supper, spy," the guard said and walked back up the stairs and shut the door.

Gordon looked at the food and began to eat. He hadn't eaten all day so this was a delicacy. He was so hungry that he licked the plate clean. And when he was done, which was only after a few minutes, he felt like Ray.

Through swollen eyes he looked up at the top of the steps and saw a light coming from under the door. There was an inch gap from the door bottom to the floor. Quietly, Gordon snuck up the steps. Every now and then his shackles hit the wooden step making a noise that made him cringe.

He laid his head sideways to look under the door; he only saw their legs. But across the room, the front door opened and in walked a man who looked exactly like General Hancock. Captain Hazard was right behind him. He dusted himself off with his gloves, while the aide held the door.

The provost marshal, Major Howard, jumped up with a surprised look on his face. He stood up and saluted. Gordon tried really hard to listen.

"To what do I owe this pleasure, General?" The marshal asked.

"Hello, Howard. I thought that I would have a little talk with the young man that can see the future," General Hancock said.

"Guards, bring the lunatic up here," Major Howard ordered.

"Have a seat, would you, General? You too, Captain Hazard."

The General sat in the seat to the right of the desk and Captain Hazard took the seat to the left.

"Make yourself at home," Howard said as he sat down behind his desk.

Gordon saw the guards coming, but before he had a chance to get back down the steps the guard opened the door.

"What do you think you're doing?" The guard was surprised to see Gordon at the top step. "Come on, the General wants to see you."

Gordon got a sick feeling in his stomach after having been caught. He was helped up by the guard and walked into the parlor. He stood there and glared across the room. "It's really you," Gordon said to Hancock.

"Have a seat, son," General Hancock said. "So far, you've been correct about the fighting in and around the rocky hill and valley area. You were also right about the fighting in the peach orchard and the wheat field. I guess that's the ones you're talking about. So the question is: How did you know all that?" Hancock asked.

"I'm not a spy. I swear," Gordon reiterated.

"Then what are you? Who are you?" General Hancock asked.

Gordon knew he was in deep trouble trying to explain something that even he didn't understand. But with his back against the wall, he figured the truth couldn't make it any worse. "I don't belong here. I mean, in this time. I'm from the..." Gordon hesitated, and then it just popped out. "Future."

"What! He's crazy," Major Howard said.

Gordon knew before he said it how dumb that sounded, but he felt he had no choice.

"Do you have proof of this claim?" Hancock on the other hand, seemed intrigued.

Gordon thought to bring up his history book, but realized it wasn't found. "No, Sir," Gordon said.

"Okay son, let me make this easer," Hancock said. "What will the Confederates do next?"

Gordon thought a moment.

"We're waiting," General Hancock said.

"The Confederates will hit the center of the Union forces tomorrow. They will break through at the rock wall where Battery A, Fourth U.S. Artillery is located. I suggest you have General Webb bring up reinforcements."

"Is this the part of your story where Lieutenant Cushing gets killed?" Major Howard asked.

"It's already written in history," Gordon replied.

General Hancock studied his face, seemingly for any deception. He was visibly troubled by this fortune teller. "You and I both know you're not from the future. But you did have good information. The problem is, are you a double agent? You do know they want to hang you?"

"I heard," Gordon said.

"But, if you can supply me with good information and it pans out, I'm sure the marshal here can spare your life."

"There's more proof, general. In his desk," Gordon said, pointing at the provost marshal's desk.

Hancock turned his attention to Major Howard. "Did you get any personal effects off the prisoner?"

Howard opened the top desk drawer slowly. He did not seem to want to share this information. He started to look through its contents and pulled out a small box with Gordon's belongings. He hesitated and then handed it to Captain Hazard, who began to look through it.

Hancock was waiting and Major Howard started to sweat. They all waited for Captain Hazard to divulge the contents.

"Like I said, General, He's crazy as a June-bug," Major Howard said in hope of discrediting what would be found.

"So, what is this stuff?" Captain Hazard asked holding up the shiny brass commemorative medal.

"I don't know, I didn't look at it," Howard said.

"Look at the year," Gordon said thinking that should have proved he was telling the truth.

Captain Hazard looked, "Let's see... 150th ... 2013."

"So what? Anyone can stamp out a fake coin," Howard said defensively.

"And this? How do you explain this?" Captain Hazard held up Gordon's laminated driver's license.

"An anomaly," Howard said.

"Anomaly, my ass! How do you explain laminates in 1863?" Gordon challenge.

"What the hell is laminates?" Major Howard asked.

Gordon heaved a sigh. He didn't know what else to say.

"It does have his likeness on it," Captain Hazard said.

"Parlor tricks, so what," Major Howard said.

"So what? It has coloring to it, somehow." Captain Hazard rubbed it. "It says here, driver's license, Ohio. Has a date on it, too. You did not find that strange? Can you guess what the date is, Howard?"

"I didn't look."

"2010," Captain Hazard said.

"Let me see that," General Hancock said.

"Like I said, anyone can make anything nowadays," Major Howard said.

"And, is this money?" Captain Hazard held up a fifty dollar bill.

"Now, that I did look at, but it was the worst counterfeit job I ever seen; it even has General Grant's likeness on it. Now, look at that date," Major Howard said.

Captain Hazard held it up to the light. "2008."

"Absurd," Major Howard said. "Nobody would take that for real money."

"Explain the color and the details in the bill," Gordon said.

General Hancock sat back in his chair. "How do you explain all of this, son?" He asked Gordon in a fatherly manor.

"I told you already, I'm from the future, and I'm a reenactor. I came here with my two friends, Mike and Ray.

That stuff on the table is mine. And for your information, that is real money where I come from."

"Howard, with your permission, I would like to take this young man with me. I'll have him by my side in the morning. If he is really from the future—"

"You're not serious, General?" Howard exclaimed.

"Wait a minute, Howard, psychic or spy, if he has information, I want him by my side."

"As you wish, General," Howard said, knowing arguing was futile.

"Son, can I trust you?" Hancock asked in earnest.

"Oh yes, General, you have my word," Gordon said with renewed life; the promise of freedom was overwhelming.

"Guards, take the shackles and handcuffs off my aide. Then clean him up; I can't have one of my aides looking like this for God's sake."

"Not a good idea, General," Howard said.

"He gave his word, Howard."

"His word... how do you know his word is any good?"

"Howard, just do what I ask."

Howard looked at the general for a moment. "You're the general," Howard nodded to the guards to take off the irons.

The guard unlocked the shackles and Gordon gave a sigh of relief. "Thank you, sir."

Gordon was allowed to wash his face in the basin, and with a wet towel, he wiped gently around his eyes, removing the hardened blood. His nose was still sensitive to the touch, but he washed it anyway. He wiped up around his ears and hair until the bowl of water turned to blood.

"Your job is to let me know, immediately, if not sooner, any information on the upcoming battle," Hancock told Gordon as he watched him clean up.

"Yes, yes, any information at all, sir," Gordon said while bent over the basin.

When Gordon was done, Hancock motioned to his new aide that it was time to go.

"Please, General, take two guards with you, just to be safe," Howard pleaded.

"Okay, Howard, if it will ease your mind."

General Hancock, followed by Captain Hazard, walked out to the front porch. When the guard escorted Gordon through the door, the General's real aide stopped Gordon by grabbing his arm. "Remember, boy, I'm keeping my eye on you."

Chapter Fourteen

July 3, 1863 - 4:30 A.M.

After leaving Sarah's house, Mike and Ray began walking through the dark woods; this time there was no moonlight. Their eyes adjusted somewhat to the darkness.

"So, you're telling me that we came through time because of some spell?"

"Yes, Ray, the poem Gordon read from the tinderbox sent us back in time. Jake was the guy that nurse hit outside the barn."

Ray's eyes lit up. "Oh, so who was the dead guy in the hayloft?"

"Must have been Earl."

"And now, we're supposed to stop this Jake guy from using the spell because he wants to escape to our future?"

"Correct again, my friend. Don't forget Earl; he's with him too. And once we have the tinderbox we can use the spell to go home. Got it?"

"I think so," Ray said.

They walked until they came to a stream. Mike could hear the crackling of musket fire in the distance. He sat down along the bank of the stream and started to take off his shoes and socks.

"Whatta ya doing Mike?" Ray asked.

"Musket fire, time to cross this stream," Mike said.

"Cross the stream?"

Mike continued taking his socks off and stood up. "You ready?"

"No," Ray said angrily. "That's the direction of the fighting."

Mike started to cross without him.

"Wait up," Ray said and entered the water.

They carried their shoes and socks, but the bottom of their pants got wet from the knee down. When they reached the other side they put their footwear back on their dirty, wet feet.

"Since gunfire is in that direction, we'll go this way," Mike said.

They continued to walk until the path became dense with the growth of underbrush. They were hitting and smacking their way through the brush the best they could when they came to a clearing.

Ray was complaining when Mike noticed a picket up ahead. Mike put up his hand to stop Ray from talking and pointed to the man. Ray quieted down.

"I got a plan," Mike said.

"Plan? What plan? You always have a plan," Ray said.

Mike crept up to the picket and saw that the man was asleep.

"Wake up, you fool," Mike whispered.

The startled picket, now terrified, desperately grabbed for his rifle.

Mike had to restrain him.

"Wait, don't kill me, I'm a friend of yours," the confused picket cried out in an attempt to save his own life.

Mike put his hand over the picket's mouth and shushed him.

"Don't hurt me," the frightened picket mumbled through Mike's hand.

"We're not going to hurt you. We're coming back from the field hospital and found you sleeping." Mike removed his hand from the picket's mouth, and held up the papers and waved them in his face. "What if the corporal had found you asleep instead of us?"

"You ain't gonna to tell him, is ya?" He asked. "I don't need that kind of trouble."

"Don't worry, we won't say a word. We just need to get back and rejoin our company," Mike said.

"Okay, who you with?" the picket asked with a soft voice. Then he swallowed.

"The Ninth Virginia, Company B," Mike said.

"You know how this works, right? I'm a gonna have to call Corporal Shepard over here," the sentry explained.

"Do what you got to do," Mike said.

"Corporal of the Guard," The young picket yelled.

The corporal appeared. "What's going on, Vernon?" He asked.

"These two approached our line, Shep. They be with the Ninth Virginia, Company B," Vernon said nervously.

"Where's your papers?" Corporal Sheppard asked.

Mike handed Sarah's forged documents over to the corporal. The corporal looked them over. "Sergeant of the guard," he yelled.

After a few minutes, the sergeant showed up.

"Sergeant, these two say they're with the Ninth. They have papers." Corporal Sheppard handed him the papers.

The sergeant looked over the documents. The sergeant let out a sigh and then threw the papers on the ground.

"Arrest them," the sergeant said. "Corporal, take these two back to camp."

"Go 'head, arrest us," Mike told the sergeant.

Corporal Sheppard, a wise older man looked at Mike as if he were mad.

"What are you doing?" Ray snapped.

"It's okay Ray, we won't have to fight if we're locked up," Mike said.

"We'll see 'bout that," the sergeant said.

He, Corporal Sheppard, and four other guards marched Mike and Ray back to camp. Mike heard the sound of wood being chopped in the distance. The camp, located on a slope nestled behind a long tree line, came into view as the bugler sounded reveille.

"I'll be damned," Mike said. He was looking directly at the flag of the 9th Virginia Volunteer Infantry Regiment. The sergeant walked them to the tent of the first sergeant of company B.

A bull of a man walked out from the tent. He wore his sun-bleached gray jacket unbuttoned. He walked up to the sergeant of the guard and sniffed at the air. "Is that perfume?

He sniffed again, "Lavender, who wears perfume and who are these two dandies?"

"They tried to cross our picket line, First Sergeant," the sergeant of the guard said.

"The rear picket line? Who crosses at the rear?" The sergeant sniffed the air by them. "You French?"

Mike and Ray just stood there. The first sergeant seemed confused, then leaned in about six inches from Ray's face and said, "Well, I'm waiting."

"Waiting for what?" Ray asked. He turned his head trying to avoid the smell of whiskey and tobacco on the first sergeant's breath.

"If you're not French, why you smell like a French whore? Why did you try to cross my picket line? And you will address me as First Sergeant! Understand?"

"We're with company B, and we're just back from the field hospital, First Sergeant," Ray said nervously.

"That's better. Where's your papers?"

"He threw them away," Ray said.

"He threw them away, First Sergeant. Who threw them away?"

"He did, First Sergeant," Ray pointed to the sergeant of the guard.

The first sergeant inclined his head and pulled back then looked at Mike. "And what's your story?"

"Trying to get arrested for Christ sakes," Mike said.

"Why?" The first sergeant was amazed.

"What's a guy got to do to get arrested around here?" Mike said.

Ray's knees buckled.

"Guard, lock them up with the rest of the prisoners. We can sort this out later."

"Yes, First Sergeant."

Vernon, the sentry that Mike had woken while on picket duty, walked up to the first sergeant. "Here, First Sergeant, the papers they lost."

The first sergeant looked over the papers. "Belay that order, this does explain things, survivors from yesterday's fight... blah, blah... being reassigned... blah, blah, blah. Sergeant what is this? You two are very lucky that I'm in a good mood."

"Shit," Mike mumbled.

"Sergeant, can you explain the discrepancy," the first sergeant asked.

"Thought they were stragglers," the sergeant of the guard said. He didn't quite know how to explain his position.

"Play-outs or stragglers, don't let me hear about you throwing papers away again. I can use all the help I can get."

"Yes, First Sergeant, won't happen again."

The first sergeant turned his attention to Mike and Ray. "Captain Wilson is having an officer's meeting now. I'm First Sergeant Roy Monroe. Give me you're names and I'll add them to the roll and give him this when he gets back."

Mike and Ray gave him their names and the first sergeant wrote them down on his small pad.

"Go with Private Vernon here and get your butts over there with the rest of the men for roll call before I put your sorry asses in company Q."

Mike and Ray turned to get to the ranks when the first sergeant noticed that they had no leather gear, haversacks, canteens, or rifles. "Where's your arms and accoutrements?"

"We have none, First Sergeant," Mike said.

"We're gonna need to replace 'em," the sergeant said directly to Mike.

"Yes sir, First Sergeant," Mike replied.

"We'll get you fixed up after roll... Private Vernon, find them haversacks and canteens," the first sergeant told them.

"Yes, First Sergeant," Vernon answered.

Mike and Ray walked over to where the company was already falling in. When Vernon got out of hearing distance Ray turned to Mike and asked, "What the hell are you doing? Are you trying to get us killed?"

"I didn't have time to tell you Ray, but when that sergeant threw our papers on the ground I thought, if we get arrested, we'll miss the charge."

"How will we get to the barn then?" Ray asked.

"We'll escape."

When they got to the company Mike stood next to Vernon. Ray stared at the men's sunburned faces, sunken cheeks, and famine-glazed eyes.

Ray got a whiff of body odor and urine. "Damn, Mike, these guys have the hygiene habits of hillbillies."

Before Ray could figure out where he was to fit into line, First Sergeant Monroe walked up behind him and yelled in his ear, "Fall in at the shoulder - pretend you have arms."

Ray was startled. He had no idea to whom to fall in on. He's always slept through drill at the reenactments and did not know these people, so he decided to stand beside Mike.

Monroe looked directly at Ray and yelled. "Short to tall, short to tall. Come on you, get in there."

Ray could feel the soldier's hot breath on his neck as Monroe pulled Ray's jacket and bodily moved him to a more appropriate place in line.

"There, that ought to do it."

Some of the men in the company began to laugh.

"Quiet in the ranks," First Sergeant Monroe yelled.

The laughter quieted. Ray was not accustomed to this kind of treatment but obeyed out of complete fear.

First Sergeant Monroe then loudly, in a deep voice, took the roll. The captain was standing at the company front. Sergeant Monroe walked to him and told him, "All men are present and accounted for, sir."

The captain turned to his company. He was a tall, stately man whose look alone demanded respect. He had the command presence and demeanor that Mike liked.

"Attention to orders: The army was engaged in a battle that we were not totally prepared for, but the early reports say that we were successful in driving the Federals from the field several times yesterday and won the day.

We have taken up a position behind Seminary Ridge to prepare ourselves for an assault on the Union center. We are no longer in reserve; we are now at the front. We will be moving out after breakfast. Break ranks, march!"

"Huz-zah," the usual cheer for breaking ranks was raised. With that, the men faced right, broke ranks, and relaxed and started mumbling as they walked toward their fire pit. Mike walked over to Sergeant Monroe. "Hey Sergeant, who is... What is the captain's name?"

"Why that's Captain John P. Wilson, Jr. What's it to you?"

"Nothing, just wanted to know, thanks sergeant."

Sergeant Monroe walked away.

"When's Pickett's Charge?" Ray asked of Mike.

"About one."

"What time is it now?"

"About six," Mike said looking at his pocket watch. Mike was weary from the morning's journey. He sniffed the air and began to walk away from Ray.

"That gives us... Mike where you going? Wait up."

Ray caught up with him. "That gives us seven hours to come up with a plan on how to get out of this mess."

Mike didn't want to think or hear about Ray's plan. He kept walking and pointed to the men cooking breakfast. "Wait up," Ray said.

Chapter Fifteen

July 3, 1863 - 6:07 A.M.
The smell of bacon cooking overrode any apprehension Mike might have had about the upcoming battle. He walked over to where the men were brewing coffee. "Morning," Mike said. The soldiers, busy with breakfast, did not return his salutation.

Private Vernon filled a sock with coffee beans, hammered it with a rock, and dropped the sock full of crushed beans into a boiling pot of dirty looking water.

"Did you see that, Mike?" Ray asked.

Mike didn't care how they made coffee. "I want to thank you for earlier," Mike said to Vernon.

"Believe in fair play, 'tis all."

Another man was cooking big slabs of bacon using a fork to flip them in the pan. He was soaking hardtack in a tin cup full of water. When the bacon was ready he removed the bacon to a tin plate. He took the hardtack from the cup and placed it in the grease of the bacon. The hardtack sizzled in the pan, soaking up the bacon grease. He then cut the cracker in half and placed a slice of bacon between the halves.

They all were ready to enjoy their morning feast of hardtack, bacon, and coffee. They sipped their coffee and stuffed the crackers, dripping with grease, into their mouths. Mike and Ray watched with their mouths agape.

After being ignored, Mike looked at Vernon for approval and picked up the pot of coffee and poured a cup for him and Ray.

"Name's John Vernon. Everyone here just calls me Vernon." He was a likeable fellow with brown hair and a little patch of hair under his lower lip.

"Good to know ya," Mike said as he leaned over the pan and took only one cracker and bacon. Then, Ray leaned over and took two from the plate. Vernon gave him a stern look.

Ray paid him no mind and took a sip of coffee and burned his lips on the hot tin cup. "Ouch, God damn it, burned myself." When he finally did taste the brew he cringed. "Now I know why they call it swamp water," Ray said.

Vernon and the other soldiers glared at him.

Ray saw them watching him, and took another sip. "I can drink this, it's good, see?" He sipped it again.

Vernon looked directly at Mike. "You should be more careful who you pick for friends. My pappy used to say, tell me who your friends are, I'll tell you who you are."

"He's all right, leave him alone. We've been through a lot."

"We've all been through a lot," Vernon said.

"Don't you think I know that?" Mike said angrily.

"Alright, alright, don't have to go and get all ignorant on me," Vernon said and backed off.

Mike felt badly that he had gotten mad. He knew they had been though more hell then he ever could imagine. He looked around at their weather-beaten faces, all looking back at him. Lips cracked from the heat. They looked to be on the verge of malnutrition. *Poor bastards are probably eating what's left of their rations.*

Ray didn't let the bad taste stand in his way any longer. "This is actually good," he said as the grease ran down his chin.

John Vernon seemed shocked, even angry at Ray's rudeness. But there was one soldier that appeared angrier than the others. He was a sulky looking man with a thin face and stone black eyes. He had a cold, menacing stare. He got up from his camp chair, walked up to Ray, and stood in front of him. "Hey, hog, where's your rifle?" He asked.

"What's it to you?" Ray asked, licking his fingers.

"Ya'll here know it, but I'll say it: ya'll deserters. Ya'll don't have your arms because ya'll threw them down and ran like the stinkin' little cowards you are."

Ray momentarily forgot himself and stood up. Then he muttered as he sat back down, "You can kiss my ass."

"What did you just say to me?"

"Leave him alone, Eli," The corporal said.

"Stay out of this, Shep. I asked you what you said."

"You heard me; and who you calling a coward?" Ray said.

"You! That's who." Eli said.

Mike was caught off guard. *These poor bastards aren't really going to fight, are they?*

Unbeknownst to Mike, Ray's brain began to steam as he got up from his seat and stood face to face with Eli, "I was just trying not to get physical, but if you really want, I'll kick your ass for ya."

"I can whip you with one arm tied behind my back. You're nut'in but a scoundrel, liar, and a coward!"

"Call me a coward, again," Ray steamed.

"I'll spell it fer ya, K-O-W...W...whatever."

When Ray's eyes met Eli's, he could see a wild-eyed, scruffy looking crazy man. He felt a momentary chill run down his spine. He passively started to sit back down, but managed to mumble, "Asshole."

As the word left Ray's lips, his head vaulted backwards as hard as a fist could hit it. Ray stumbled to the ground holding his jaw.

"Hope ya fight as well as ya talk!" Eli warned.

Mike jumped up from his seat. Eli looked at his size and said, "Wait your turn."

Ray shook it off and got up. "It's okay, Mike."

"No, it's not," Mike said.

The other men gathered for a good fight. Eli looked around as an audience gathered.

"Don't worry, Mike. I can take this dumbass hillbilly," Ray reassured him.

Ray walked into another fist when the word hillbilly left his mouth. Ray was down on the ground again, rubbing his jaw.

"Who you calling hillbilly?" Eli warned.

Mike started to get between the two men when the corporal grabbed him. "Let them go, that friend of yours needs to grow up a bit."

Mike thought about it a moment and then relaxed. "Maybe we'll get locked up after all," Mike said as he sat back down and waited.

Ray looked around for Mike to rescue him, but Mike didn't move from his seat.

"Okay then, I'm okay." He turned back around to meet Eli's fist for the third time. It connected like a brick on Ray's lower jaw. Ray was startled; he thought his jaw was broken. Then, out of instinct, Ray swung back like a wild man. Two, then three swings later, he finally hit Eli in the jaw.

The other soldiers were now taking bets on who would win this contest, playing one against the other as they were heard yelling, "Give him a good licking Eli, that boy fights like a girl."

Eli stepped on Ray's foot, pinning it to the ground. Ray, with his foot held, couldn't retreat. Eli cocked his fist back and let go, punching Ray in the mouth again. Ray went down.

Eli quickly jumped on Ray and held him to the ground. "Give up now?" Eli asked.

"That's enough, I'm stopping the fight," Mike said.

"No!" Ray yelled, barely moving with Eli holding him down.

"That there boy sure is bullheaded," Vernon said.

"A smart man knows when to give up," said a soldier with money riding on Eli.

"Where's your horse sense boy? Give it up," another yelled.

"If you've had enough, I'll let ya up." Eli said.

Ray, still on the ground, looked through the blood and dirt in his eyes and like a school kid said, "I'll stop, if you'll stop."

Mike grabbed Eli and pulled him off Ray and then threw him to the ground. Eli scrambled to his feet and said. "You sum-bitch, I'll break your neck."

"Here's my neck, break it," Mike said.

Eli didn't know quite what to do: fight or retreat. He just stood there.

"You'll all stop now," First Sergeant Monroe threatened as he walked over. The corporal, seeing Monroe, got between Mike and Eli.

"Save it for the Yankees," Monroe said.

"Where the hell you been?" Eli asked.

"Apologize, *now!*" Monroe ordered.

"Sure sergeant, which one?" Eli asked.

"Jesus Christ, Eli, how many were you fightin'?" Sergeant Monroe asked.

Eli seemed grateful the fight was over and agreed to apologize. He walked to Ray. "Here, let me help you up." Eli held out his hand in a gesture of goodwill.

Ray took his hand cautiously and let Eli help him up. Eli dusted himself off and slowly walked away with Vernon and his fellow pards as they cashed in their bets.

First Sergeant Monroe grabbed Ray by the coat and manhandled him over to the corporal. Ray thought he was going to get his ass beaten again, only this time by the sergeant.

"Corporal Sheppard, take these two over to the ordinance wagon to get leather gear and rifles with enough rounds for a good fight. Tell him Roy sent ya," He said, holding a slip of paper with the orders written on it.

"Yes, First Sergeant, consider it done."

Then the sergeant glared at Ray from the shadow of his hat brim. "Consider yourself on report. Next infraction and I'll place the both of you with the rest of the misfits."

Ray looked at Mike through the blood in his eyes. Mike, lost for words, only shook his head.

"Let's go, boys, and get you fixed up," Corporal Sheppard said.

Chapter Sixteen

Friday, July 3, 1863 - 8:01 A.M.

For the first time in two days, Gordon awoke to daylight and the birds chirping. It felt good even though there was shelling and musket fire in the distance that had started five in the morning. He was in a tent shelter with two soldiers standing guard. "General said you could sleep in. Don't think he meant all day. Get up."

Gordon crawled out from the shelter and found himself in the front yard of a farm house. "Who could sleep with all this noise? Could you tell them to turn it down a bit?" he said with a smile. He looked down at the wet grass: it looked greener.

Gordon took in a deep breath and then let it out. His ribs felt better. He could smell the sulfur from the spent gunpowder. The Confederates had been trying to take Culp's Hill all morning with heavy skirmishing.

Gordon felt dried blood in his hair that he had missed while cleaning up. His swollen eyes stung from the smoke drifting along the fields, and his wrists were sore from the heavy steel handcuffs that had cut into his skin. "God damn, look what they did."

The guards allowed Gordon to stretch and get the morning kinks out. Gordon was standing just behind Cemetery Ridge watching the horses and mule teams pull the wagons everywhere. He heard shouting in the distance and looked around the yard. He had to shelter his eyes from the strong sunlight.

He saw a soldier carrying a live rooster in each hand. Another man calmly chopped their heads off with a hatchet and then threw them in a cauldron of boiling water.

Another soldier pulled them out of the boiling water and started plucking the feathers, preparing them for stew. Gordon felt badly for the rooster, but knew the men had to eat, and this was how man got a chicken sandwich before McDonald's was around.

A runner appeared from over the hill and ran past several men carrying firewood. The runner met the corporal and handed him a note. The runner waited for a reply, but the corporal just stared at the note.

"What's it mean? I can't read that good."

"Can't read that good myself," Gordon overheard the runner say. "May I?" Gordon offered.

The corporal handed Gordon the note. He studied it a moment.

"What's it say?" the corporal asked.

"Looks like the General wants the clairvoyant at his side," Gordon said.

"Clair-a-what?"

"Me," Gordon said and handed the note back.

Gordon was glad the General wanted to see him, but he thought that too much information could be bad. He didn't want to change history. He looked at the corporal. "I'm ready."

As they walked, Gordon could see and hear the activity of the men scrambling on Cemetery Hill. They were placing batteries of cannons there. The guard moved Gordon to the right to let the infantry march by. With the temperature rising, the odor the men were emitting was becoming obnoxious.

They walked along the Ridge toward Cemetery Hill. To Gordon's left was the stone wall leading to the Angle. Gordon couldn't make out the exact units, but he knew that Pennsylvania men were stationed at that part of the field.

As the guard walked along following the wagon ruts, it dawned on Gordon: *We're walking along what will become Hancock Avenue.* He shook his head in disbelief.

Then he realized that the muskets and cannons were not firing any longer. Not a sound could be heard. Gordon looked up toward the sky and saw white, fleecy clouds floating by. Gordon remembered: there was supposed to be a dead silence that came over the field prior to the storm.

The guards walked Gordon over to where General Hancock was busy discussing tactics with Brigadier General John Gibbon and Colonel Wheelock Veazey of the 16th Vermont; Gordon recognized them from the many books he had read.

While they waited for Hancock, Gordon looked around. A few yards away there were the wounded: Union and Confederate. He glanced over and saw the wounded being brought in on stretchers to an aid station. Over the moans he heard the voice of General Hancock.

"Good morning, Mister Smart," Hancock said.

"Good morning to you, General."

"Already hot this morning. Are they treating you well?

"Yes, sir," Gordon said.

"Today, you'll prove yourself loyal, right? Don't make me shoot you in this heat." A slight smile came across the general's face.

"Oh, yes, General, I'm a loyal Union man alright. And that's the way I'm going to keep it," Gordon said.

"Did you think of anything important during the night?"

"Yes, sir, that's all I've been thinking about."

"Well, let's hear it, damn it."

"Well, General, the Confederates will hit the center of the Union line, immediately following the cannonade."

"Christ sakes, you don't have to be clairvoyant to know that!" Hancock said. "So what about it?"

"At one o'clock, one of the greatest artillery duels on the continent will begin," Gordon explained with a gleam in his eye.

"What about the center?" Hancock asked.

"You see that clump of trees over there? That's where the rebs will focus their attack this afternoon."

"Christ, don't tell me that's all you got," General Hancock looked at his watch, "Close to nine, which gives us about four hours... Tell me you have something else?"

Gordon was thinking quickly and getting nervous. "Well, you might want to move the supply train farther back."

"What the hell are you talking about? The wagons are a mile back, why would they be in any danger?"

"Confederate cannons will overshoot your front lines and hit the train."

"You sure about this?"

"Very sure,"

"You're telling me that they'll miss our front lines?"

"Correct, for the most part," Gordon said. "There is another thing."

"What?" Hancock asked, getting annoyed.

"The Confederates will send cavalry to break through your rear lines."

"That's a given, do you have a location?"

"Spangler's Spring," Gordon said.

"You're very sure of yourself, aren't you?" Hancock asked.

"Yes, sir, I am," Gordon said.

"Well, I'm not," Hancock said. He motioned to his aide to come to him. "Bring me my horse and have Captain Hazard come here."

"Yes, sir," the aide said as he left.

General Hancock became very thoughtful and put his right hand to his goatee and stroked at it. "I was going to shoot you yesterday, now I'm supposed to trust you this morning. I'll think on it, if you don't mind."

"I know my history, General."

"Well, someone taught you tactics, that's for sure."

Gordon stopped short of telling General Hancock that he, too, would fall that day, and lose an arm. The aide and Captain Hazard returned with the general's horse.

"I'm placing this man under your command. He's proven himself loyal."

"Yes, sir," Captain Hazard said.

"Now, I've got to go and figure out how to present this new information to General Meade and his staff."

"If there is anyone who could make him understand, it's you, General," Captain Hazard said.

Hancock mounted his black charger, pulled on the reins and turned and said, "Wish me luck." Then he kicked the animal and galloped off toward Meade's headquarters.

"I'm assigning you to Lieutenant Cushing," Captain Hazard said. "The guard will escort you there."

"Yes, sir," Gordon said.

The guard led Gordon past the wounded and continued their walk down to where Battery A of the Fourth U.S. Light Artillery Regiment was located, right behind the dreaded angle.

When they got there Gordon was awestruck. As he gazed upon the field, he put aside the appalling picture of the wounded. Now, he was focused on the real Cushing's battery. Only in his wildest dreams could he fathom actually being here. Now, he didn't care how he got here. In his mind, he had a front row seat to the greatest battle of all time: Pickett's Charge. He would get to see, first hand, the three divisions march across that mile-long field and walk right up in front of the guns of the Forth U.S. Artillery.

Just then, Gordon saw Alonzo Hereford Cushing light up his meerschaum pipe and sit down behind one of the guns. Sergeant Frederick Fuger handed him a coffee. Second Lieutenant Joseph Milne was also sitting there. They were eating some pork and hard crackers. Gordon recognized them from the history books. *I could be watching Cushing's last meal*, he thought.

Some foot soldiers walked over and cheerfully greeted them and sat down for a late breakfast. While Gordon was in a flight of imagination, Lieutenant Cushing approached and introduced himself. "Remember me? The one you wanted to kill?"

"Yes, I do, Lieutenant, but I never wanted to kill you, sir."

"The General might trust you, but I don't. That begs the question of what to do with you," Cushing said.

"Sir?" Gordon said as he swallowed.

"Guards, shackle him to the limber," Lieutenant Cushing ordered.

Gordon was mortified. He knew the cannonade was coming and—without the freedom to move—he would be a sitting duck.

"Are you right-handed or left-handed?" The guard asked.

"Right-handed, but what does that have to do with anything?" Gordon asked.

"This," the guard said as he shackled his right hand to the wheel.

Gordon struggled. He saw the crew posted beside their gun. He saw the man who may have been his great-great-grandfather, Mortimer, standing there. He was the same handsome young man he had seen earlier at the provost marshal's office. Gordon needed to make him understand that he was no threat.

Standing there, shackled to the wheel, Gordon began to think of what to say to get out of this predicament. When he couldn't come up with a good reason, his stomach tightened again.

Chapter Seventeen

Friday, July 3, 1863 - 7:03 A.M.

"Tell 'em Roy sent ya, huh?" Corporal Leon Sheppard repeated the words of First Sergeant Roy Monroe. It was the order to get replacement rifles and accoutrements.

Corporal Sheppard turned to Mike and Ray. "Here's a couple of haversacks and canteens fer ya. Private Vernon found them for ya."

"Thanks, corporal," Mike said.

"Shep, you can call me Shep. The ordnance wagon has come up. Now, let's go get your rifles."

"Great," Ray said.

Corporal Sheppard walked Mike and Ray down a dirt road following wagon ruts. Other soldiers past them and waved. The supply trains were about a half mile to the rear. "Look fellows, to prevent any misunderstanding with the ordnance sergeant you should just let me do all the talking."

"Sure, you're the man," Mike said.

"You talk funny, sure you're not French?" Corporal Sheppard said with a smile.

Mike knew there was a strong French influence in the Victorian era, from perfume to military tactics, including the bayonet exercise which was all based on the French drill.

They walked to the rear of the camp where several wagons came up in advance of the rest of the train. The wagons, covered with white canvas, included the subsistence stores, commissary, ordinance depot, and the quartermaster.

There was a sutler wagon that caught the blue eyes of Corporal Sheppard. Until now, the army had pilfered what they could from the farms in the area.

Sheppard's eyes lit up when he saw the sutler wagon. "Look, you fellows take this note and go over to the ordinance wagon and get your stuff. I'll be right over. Let me go over here and pay a little visit to these thieves." Corporal Sheppard handed the note to Mike and then walked over to the sutler.

Mike watched him for a moment, then he and Ray walked over to the ordnance depot wagon. Ray shouted for someone to help them. "Is anybody here?"

A bear of a man stepped out from around the wagon. Ray was stunned; he didn't know what to say so he just stood there. Mike put his hand on Ray's shoulder. "Let me do the talking."

The bear was a sergeant. He stared down at Ray with his hands on his waist. "So, what can I do fer ya?" He said in a raspy voice.

"We're here for guns and ammo," Mike said.

The sergeant drew back and then with a hard look said, "Sergeant!"

Mike quickly restated the question, "We came to get guns and ammo, sergeant."

"And why should I give you my guns and ammo?" The sergeant said.

"The hospital lost ours," Mike lied.

"Well then, why should I give you more equipment? So you can lose them too!"

Sheppard appeared with his calm southern drawl and said, "The fact still remains, Jim, they don't have any rifles or rounds. No equipment at all for a fight. They will be of very little help without weapons, won't they? Besides they have a note from First Sergeant Roy Monroe of company B, he's the one that sent us."

"Where's the note?" The sergeant asked Mike.

"Oh yeah, here, sergeant" Mike handed him the note.

The sergeant began reading the note, looking at Mike ever so often. When he finished, he thought for a moment and his sourness somewhat retracted.

"How is Roy?"

"He's well," Corporal Sheppard said.

"How did you two miss the rounds being passed out this morning?" The sergeant asked.

"They just got back from the hospital, Jim." Corporal Sheppard said.

Mike noticed how Corporal Sheppard used the sergeant's first name, Jim, and that Jim didn't mind. They were on familiar ground. *They must be old friends,* Mike thought.

The sergeant reached into the wagon and started to talk, apparently to himself, while rummaging through the back of the wagon. "You're right, Shep, here's two brand new Enfield rifles and cartridge boxes with forty rounds and the cap boxes, with caps, to go with them. That ought to do it for any fight you will have in the near future. I suggest you don't lose them!"

Ray looked at his new rifle in awe. He couldn't believe he had his hands on an original issue Enfield. Only in his dreams could he afford to own one of these babies back in the real world.

"Thank you, sergeant," Ray said almost getting misty eyed. The sergeant looked at Ray and shook his head.

The sergeant looked at Mike while he, too, was examining his new Enfield rifle in awe. Then the sergeant began writing on a slip of paper as he read out loud.

"That will be twenty five cents for each round, seventeen dollars per rifle, eight dollars for the cartridge box, five dollars for the cap box, and ten dollars for the bayonet."

The sergeant then looked at them and asked. "How you two fixed on rations?"

Mike looked into his haversack. He had a tin cup, a tin plate, and a knife and fork, but nothing to eat. He looked at Ray. "What do you have, Ray?"

Ray looked through the sack carefully; he had the same. "Nut'in."

The sergeant wrote out a separate note for the subsistence store's rations and handed it to Ray. "Take this to the commissary."

"Where's that, sergeant?" Ray asked.

"Next wagon down, half-wit."

Ray was stunned—*half-wit!*—but he ignored the remark as he was more than happy with his Enfield rifle. He moved to the next wagon along with Mike and Corporal Sheppard. The sergeant came around the wagon. "Looking for me?" he laughed.

"You again?" Ray mumbled.

"Who'd you expect, your mother? I'm the only one here today. Who are these two dandies anyway, Shep?"

"Why, where's my manners? This here is Mike Hill and Ray Hensley; boys meet Sergeant Jim Biddison."

"Nice to meet ya," Mike said.

Ray looked at the note, "Why only three day's rations, sergeant?"

Sergeant Biddison's face turned sour once again as he looked at Ray as if he were a spoiled child. "That's your life expectancy!"

After he gave them hardtack and salt pork he wrote the dollar amount along with the orders on another piece of paper. When he was finished he saw that Ray had his hand out for it. He gave the paper to Corporal Sheppard instead. "Be sure Roy gets this, Shep."

"I wanted to read it," Ray said.

Corporal Sheppard, staring at Ray, slipped the paper in his pocket.

"Thanks Jim," Sheppard said, then grabbed Ray by the arm and led him away. Mike turned and joined them.

As they walked back across the dust covered road they passed more soldiers walking to and fro. Sheppard took out the orders and paraphrased the contents. "Your pay will be held until your new equipment is paid off."

Ray grinned. "What! We get paid? Wow, that's a nice surprise."

Corporal Sheppard looked confused at Ray. "I said you're not getting paid."

Ray changed his bright outlook to his more usual miserable self. "Oh, you mean we're not getting paid, bummer."

"What does foraging have to do with it? Never mind, I don't want to know. There's more," Corporal Sheppard added. "You'll be placed on extra duty also."

"What extra duty?" Now Ray got serious.

"Come on, let's hear it," Mike said.

"I'll tell ya, but you won't like it. The other duty will be to go out on the field after the battle and pick up all the unused cartridges that you can find -"

"What's so bad about that?" Ray interrupted.

"Off the dead, friend or foe. This is to re-supply what ya'll took today."

Ray was beside himself. "I can't believe this shit! I won't do it! They can't make me do that!"

"Dems the rules: when a private loses his equipment he is charged for said lost equipment. Plus he has to do extra duty, that's just the way it is, boys. That order went into effect after the first year of the war. I'm surprised that you don't know that," Corporal Sheppard explained.

"Don't worry about it, Ray, because we won't be here," Mike whispered to Ray.

When they finally got back to camp First Sergeant Roy Monroe was waiting for them. Corporal Sheppard spied the sergeant and walked directly to him. He handed over the orders from Sergeant Biddison. First Sergeant Monroe studied them.

"Join the ranks; I'll deal with this later."

Mike looked at his grandfather's watch; it was just after eight o'clock. Mike and Ray quickly donned their accoutrements and joined the ranks. The men were already standing at attention when Mike and Ray got in line.

First Sergeant Monroe was now facing the first lieutenant at the front of the company. "All men are present and accounted for, sir," Monroe barked.

Captain John P. Wilson, Jr. was a tall, stately man with a stern look. Mike took notice of his stony green eyes and jet black hair that stuck out from under his gray kepi. The captain topped the look off with a Van Dyck style beard.

"Attention Company, attention to orders. Today our regiment will be with General Armistead's brigade and will be part of General Pickett's Division."

Cheers filled the sky; the men seemed to be thrilled. Mike and Ray exchanged glances. Mike had read about the men cheering, but to witness the response firsthand was overwhelming. He got caught up in it and cheered along with them.

When the cheering calmed down Captain Wilson went on. "We will hit the center of the Federal line where the enemy is weakest. Attention to these next orders: all commanders are authorized to order the instant death of any soldier who fails in his duty at this hour. I hope each and every one of you understands the consequences of your actions. That is all, gentlemen." Captain Wilson paused, and with an afterthought added, "With this heat, I want full canteens out there. We will form up shortly, break ranks, marrrch."

The men hollered, "Huz Zah," faced right, and broke ranks.

Ray's mind raced. "I was thinking, Mike. Since we... well, you know the history, let's give General Lee his climatic battle and win the day."

Mike pulled Ray away from the eavesdroppers.

"What are you talking about?"

"Let's tell the first sergeant that we have an urgent message for General Lee."

"What urgent message?" Mike asked.

"Well, General Lee thinks the Yankee army is far to the rear, right? Doesn't the cannon overshoot the Yankee actual positions?"

"Yeah, where you going with this?"

"What if we write a map of the exact positions of the Yankee army, hiding behind the rock wall and all that? We can also include the correct elevation for their cannons for maximum effectiveness."

"Hummm," Mike was interested.

Chapter Eighteen

Friday, July 3, 8:52 A.M.

Mike was very interested in Ray's proposal. "We could tell Lee to support the charge with a second wave," Mike said.

"Yeah, Mike, yeah," Ray was getting excited.

"Get me a piece of paper, Ray."

Ray went running. When he got back he placed the paper on a tree stump that Mike rolled over.

"Where did you get the paper?" Mike wondered.

"Same place I got the pencil: Corporal Sheppard," he said and handed it to Mike.

Mike thought a moment. "Along with the Yankee positions, we'll also include that God damn fence along Emittsburg road." Mike started to draw. "If Lee takes that out, *wow*, a major advantage to the Confederacy. There will be a clear route all the way to the Union lines."

"That's what I'm talking about," Ray said. His excitement rose as he saw Mike draw the whole area.

"Tell him to shorten the fuses and include a converging fire from two directions upon the same area by his artillery."

"What area, Mike?"

"The Angle."

"Wow," Ray said as he watched Mike draw.

"All the while, we'll be at General Lee's headquarters directing the whole battle. And, may I add, out of harm's way," Mike said as he continued to draw.

"That's a plan, alright," Ray said.

Mike filled in the final touches.

"Our we going to tell the sergeant?"

"We are suppose to follow the chain of command," Mike corrected him.

"Well, I guess I'm ready," Ray said looking at the finished map. Then he looked up at Mike, who looked somber. "What's wrong Mike?"

"You know we can't do this, right?"

Ray nodded his head that he understood. As a warm breeze blow, all hopes of staying out of the fight vanished.

"It's really the only way," Mike said.

"Good plan, though."

Mike crumpled up the paper and stuffed it in his pocket. They walked back toward their company.

"All we need to do is get to the barn," Mike reminded Ray as they walked.

"Right, but how? I'm all fuzzy on the details. You know, crossing that field without getting killed and all that."

"Sarah placed a spell on us to keep us safe, remember?" Mike said.

"Yeah, right, so crossing that field is much better now?

"Just stick with me. That's all you have to do."

"Do you really think we can make it to the barn?"

"We have to," Mike said.

"We could get killed instead," Ray said.

"We have no choice. Hell, the sergeant will kill us if we don't!"

Mike and Ray wandered back just in time to help break camp. They loaded the tent fly into the wagon. Pots and pans had to be loaded along with any extra provisions they had, compliments of the farmers in the area. When they were finished packing, the soldiers poured what coffee they had left into everyone's cups, and they extinguished the fire.

Vernon poured Mike and Ray the last of the coffee and went to clean the pot.

Mike leaned toward Ray and whispered, "I've got a plan to get us home."

"Yeah, what's that?"

"Keep your voice down," Mike made a hand gesture. "There will be a depression just before the fence line. We'll wait there until the battle's over."

"Then what? Ray asked.

"When it's all over we'll wander off the field with the other soldiers and hide in the woods until dark. Then beeline it back to the barn and go home."

"What makes you think we'll make it to the fence?"

"Trust me," Mike said.

"Trust you, that's it?"

"Yeah."

"Some plan," Ray said.

Mike looked around the camp and saw that several men were writing their names on slips of paper, then pinning the slips to the inside their coats.

"I'll be damned, look at that," Mike said.

"What?"

"Don't you recognize what they're doing?"

"Hell no. Why should I?" Ray said.

"They're making dog tags."

"No shit? Maybe we should do the same."

"Lotta good that'll do us, we're a 150 years from home," Mike smiled.

"Hey Mike, can you do me a favor?"

"What's that?"

"If I don't make it—"

"Stop right there. You're not going to die," Mike said. "And I don't want to hear it again."

"Alright, don't have to get all ignorant on me," Ray said. "But—"

"But, hell," Mike said. He didn't want to think about the possibility of dying.

Ray smiled and then, absentmindedly, took out his pack of cigarettes that still had its cellophane. He shook one out. The filter end was broken and he threw it into the fire. Then he lit up another, using his Zippo.

Vernon, now sitting next to Eli, watched Ray light the perfect cylindrically-shaped cigarette. "What the hell you doing, boy?"

"Smoking a cigarette," Ray said matter-of-factly.

"We chaw where I come from," Vernon said.

"Yeah, well, we smoke," Ray said and took a drag.

"Let me have one," Vernon asked.

"I only have one," Ray said.

"Only want one," Vernon said.

"Okay, okay. Here," Ray pulled out his last cigarette and handed it to him.

"What's this cotton fer?" Vernon asked, studying the filter.

"The filter?" Ray asked.

"What's it filtering?"

"Tar and nicotine, I guess."

Vernon scratched his head. "Know what tar is. What the hell is it doing in a cigarette? And what the heck is... nic -a - what?"

"Just smoke the damn thing."

Ray leaned over with his lighter and lit the cigarette. Vernon took a long drag taking in a lot of the smoke. "Hell, you can't taste that thing." Vernon ripped the filter off the end of the cigarette and threw it in the fire. Then he took another long drag. "Shit, that still ain't noth'in." Vernon ripped the paper open and threw the tobacco in his mouth. "You should chew like a real man." Vernon cringed and spit it out on the ground. "God damn Frenchified things, ain't good fer nuth'in."

"Give me that," Mike said to Ray.

"What?"

"The cigarette package."

Ray handed Mike the cigarette package in front of Vernon. Mike crumpled it up. Vernon began to wave his hands as if he wanted to see it but Mike simply dropped it in the fire. "What ya do that fer? I wanted to look at that."

"Sorry," Mike said. He felt the need to rid the 19th Century of modern things.

Vernon now motioned for the tin that Ray used to light it. "Can I have a look see?" Vernon asked.

Ray hesitated, and then handed the Zippo lighter to Vernon. He looked it over and scratched his head. He showed it to Eli. "Ever see anything like this?"

"Naw, can't say I have," Eli said.

"Well, how do—" Vernon looked puzzled.

Ray leaned over, opened the lighter, and flicked it for him. Vernon gasped and almost fell off his seat when it lit. The other soldiers joined their little group. They sat gawking at the strange device. Grinning now, Vernon wanted to flick it himself. After a few attempts the fire started.

"What makes it catch fire?"

Ray began to explain it to him. He even took it apart to show him. Ray handed the parts over to Vernon to examine. "So, what you're saying is: this tin full of fine lamp oil, you call lighter fluid, has a cotton wick, a flint, and a metal roller. When you flick the roller, the flint makes a spark which catches the wick of fine oil on fire."

Ray didn't want to explain the lighter fluid again and thought he was close enough. "Right on," Ray said.

"Right on what?" Vernon asked, confused.

"That's right - how it works, I mean," Ray said.

"Well, I'll be."

Vernon handed the lighter parts back to Ray so he could put it together again. "You like to trade something for it?"

"Sorry, it belonged to my father."

Ray reassembled the lighter. Vernon scratched his head, and then smelled his hands. "Muh hands stinks of that shit.

Ray was about to put the lighter away when Eli grabbed it from him and handed it to Vernon.

"Thanks Eli," Vernon said then opened it and flicked the roller again and again. On the third attempt it lit and the lighter fluid on his hands caught fire.

The other soldiers were shocked and jumped away. Mike quickly took off his coat and wrapped it around Vernon's hands. Vernon started to fight Mike. "Get off me," he said as he pushed him. "Hold still," Mike yelled as he held his arms. Hats flew as they continued to wrestle. Mike let go and Vernon ripped the coat from his hands and threw it on the ground. He saw that his hands were burned, but was glad that the fire was out.

"Damn you're hard to help," Mike said picking up his hat and coat.

It wasn't a bad burn, but it was painful and Vernon didn't want to hold the strange tin any longer and threw it on the ground. The other soldiers laughed after seeing how much they all jumped.

Ray picked up the lighter. "You didn't have to do that."

"That's dangerous," Vernon said. "I don't think I want it no more."

Vernon showed the burn to Eli. "Here, lemme put some lard on it. My momma always put fat on our burns."

Mike heard what he said and interrupted. "Put water on it."

"What?" Eli said.

"Water, you put cold water on a burn," Mike said.

"Don't know nuth'in, do ya. God knows what you find in water. Shit will kill you. Everyone knows you put butter on a burn, you dumb bastard."

"Do what you want, none of my business, but lard or butter holds in the heat of the burn."

"You're right. None o' your business," Eli said.

Eli and Vernon both got up and walked away together. Ray seemed relieved when they were gone. Mike leaned towards Ray's ear and whispered, "I knew that farb shit would get you in trouble."

Mike got up to clean his plate. Ray stood up along with him. "What are we doing?"

Mike didn't answer, instead watched the other soldiers use the water from their canteens to wash their plates. They poured it in the plates and swished it around with their fingers. Then they wiped it off with grass and brushed their hands dry on their trousers. Some used the same oily towel that they used to wipe their muskets off with.

"No wonder they all got sick and died," Mike said.

Mike and Ray washed their plates and when they were finished, they walked back to the fire and set down with Eli and Vernon. They quietly sat there, all the while, Mike was trying to think of something to say, but before anyone could say anything, the drum roll started.

"First call," First Sergeant Monroe yelled. Company B stopped what they were doing and got to their feet. The rustling of tin cups began as the men put their coats on and donned their accoutrements.

"What's happening?" Ray asked with a worried look.

"We're moving out," Mike replied.

"Oh God," Ray cringed. "I don't know if I can go through with it. I'm gonna be sick, Mike." Ray's face grew uneasy. He leaned over, grabbing his stomach. Mike patted him on the back to try and ease his friend's mind.

"Don't be scared, Ray. Just stick with me."

Then Ray threw up, Mike walked in front of him to hide his sickness from the others. "Remember the plan, Ray."

"What plan?" Ray asked as he spit out the last of his vomit on the ground.

"The fence - to wait - God damn it," Mike said.

"Fall in!" First Sergeant Monroe yelled.

***

Meanwhile, deep in Pitzer's woods, Jake and Earl were hiding from both the blue and gray armies.

"We'll wait 'til after this fighting is done."

"How long will that take, Jake?" Earl asked, as he whittled on a stick.

"As long as it takes, Earl, doesn't matter, we wait here at least 'til dark. Then we'll wander down into that valley between the big boulders over yonder and make our way back to the road. Then follow it to the barn."

Earl threw the stick away and stared at the ground.

"What's wrong?"

"Just thinking about things."

"What things?"

"I feel bad we're not in the fight."

"You have a death wish?"

"I feel that I let Sarah down, too."

"You're a piece of work, Earl. All we needs to do is get the tinderbox and get out of this God-forsaken world. And with all that gold, we'll be the massa," Jake added.

Chapter Nineteen

Friday, July 3, 1863 - 10:17 A.M.
"Let's go company B, Captain Wilson is waiting on us," First Sergeant Monroe yelled.

The clamoring of equipment began as heavy footed soldiers grabbed their rifles and got into formation. The company of about 30 men fell in at the shoulder with the efficiency of the veterans that they were.

Mike and Ray were the last in line. Ray's size dictated his place in line, but due to Ray's aversion to drill at reenactments, he was confused about the whole short to tall protocol. Eli called to him. "Over here."

Ray heard him and found his place in line, but he was a platoon away from Mike.

"What's wrong with you?" Eli whispered.

Ray ignored him. The company was at shoulder arms and Ray wasn't.

"Shoulder arms, you dumb bastard," Eli said.

Ray had never practiced drill; he hated it. Now he didn't know what the orders meant. He looked to see what he was supposed to do.

Standing there at the company front, once more, was Captain John P. Wilson, Jr., the tall stately man that Mike liked when he and Ray had first gotten there.

"Attention, company! In each rank, count two!" The men began to count, "One, two, one, two," and so on down the line. When the counting was done, Ray was a two. Captain Wilson then ordered, "Company, right face." The company turned to the right. The "two man," stepped up to the "one man's," right side. Ray turned right, but didn't step up.

The second sergeant saw him. "Two's step up."

"That's you, dummy." Eli pushed Ray making him get beside his "one man."

"Forward, march!" Captain Wilson yelled.

The company stepped off briskly with files of four men abreast. Mike was next to Vernon in the first platoon and Ray was in the second, with Eli to his left. They marched elbow to elbow out to the field to join the other companies that made up the regiment.

Sergeant Monroe saw Mike get out of step. "To the *step!*" He yelled. All the men glanced down at their feet and looked to see who was out of step. "Come on, fresh fish, dress it up," Vernon said to Mike.

Captain Wilson marched his company out to where the regiment was forming up. His company was forming on the color company, the lead who were always set first. When the guides were three paces from the captain, the company halted.

"By file into line—march!" ordered Captain Wilson.

His company formed on the line of battle. Each file of the company was placed on the line before the next file moved. Ray, not knowing this, went ahead of Eli. "Where you going? I swear you must be some kind of Jonah."

"What, now I'm a jinx?"

"Guides, post!"

The file closers and guides scurried to their positions. As they ran, their trouser legs rubbed together. Their leather gear flapped along with their haversacks and canteens. They were charged with maintaining the alignments of the company.

"Support arms!" Captain Wilson gave the order to let the colonel know that his company was set and ready.

The 9th Virginia regiment was now formed and was made up of about 300 men led by Major John C. Owens; Mike recognized him from the regimental history.

Ray was glad the maneuvering was over. It was hot and the wool he was wearing was uncomfortable. "Must be ninety degrees out here," Ray said. Then he heard the field music begin.

After a few words with the other officers, Major Owens ordered, "Battalion—by company, right wheel. March!"

"Here we go again," Ray complained. He stepped on the heel of the man in front of him. "Sorry."

"Sorry, you're the sorry one."

"Do I have to watch you every minute?" Eli said.

Each company, like a fan, swung to the right and pivoted into a single column of companies, one right behind the other.

As they marched along, Mike remembered that each company acted as a unit within the regiment and that each regiment maneuvered within the brigade. He hoped that all he would have to do was follow their lead.

The dust rose high into the air from the men marching. The music helped to keep the cadence. Dirt entered Mike's mouth, nose, and ears. He pulled down his hat brim. He squinted his eyes in the bright sunlight. He heard the heavy footfalls made by the men's brogans thumping the ground as one. The clanging of tin cups seemed to dominate the air. Mike could hear the officers' sabers clanking as they walked along.

Major Owens marched his regiment out to where Brigadier General Lewis Armistead's brigade was forming up.

The regiment marched up a long grade toward the tree line just behind Seminary Ridge. When they finished their deployment Major Owens ordered, "Colors and guides, post!" Mike heard the ruffling of clothing and equipment filling the air as the brigade of about 1,500 men was formed. And there in the front, Mike recognized the 46-year-old Brigadier General Lewis Armistead.

"By columns of two, *march!*" General Armistead yelled. He marched his brigade out to where General Pickett's division was forming up just behind the tree line.

"Brigade - Halt," General Armistead ordered.

The sound of an entire brigade coming to a complete stop was surreal to Mike.

While maintaining a company front, General Lewis Armistead maneuvered his brigade In mass behind General Garnett's brigade which had moved into the wooded area. Mike looked around for General Kemper's brigade. It should've been to the right front, but he couldn't see them either. The division looked like it was half in the woods and half out.

"Guides, post!" General Armistead shouted.

More rustling was heard as the guides retired to the rear. After a few formalities with the officers, General Armistead's brigade was just behind the tree line at Seminary Ridge.

Mike remembered that there were fifteen Virginia Regiments that made up Pickett's Division and that they had fewer then 6,000 men. He had the smallest division in the Army of Northern Virginia. But in spite of these low numbers, Mike still thought this group was enormous. Even Ray was at a loss for words.

After a few words of encouragement to the men, Major Owens saluted the regiment and walked off.

"Fix bayonets," Captain Wilson ordered.

The men made little effort fixing the bayonets to the barrels of their muskets. The clanging of cold steel was heard down the line. Ray had a little trouble there, but the next order posed a bigger problem.

"Stack arms," was the next order from the captain.

After a few mishaps, Ray dropped his musket on the ground with a loud thud, and Eli picked it up and stacked it properly for him. Ray gave Eli an agreeable nod.

"The chaplain will be here shortly to give his blessing. Company, *rest!*" Captain Wilson ordered. This meant the men were not to wander far from their own stacks of arms.

Ray, not knowing that little detail, started to walk towards Mike. Eli grabbed his coat. "Where you going?" Eli asked.

"I'm just going over to Mike," Ray said.

"You know what rest means?" Eli said.

"I'm not tired," Ray said and walked over to Mike.

"Are you trying to do get us in trouble?" Mike asked Ray.

"This shit is getting old, quick," Ray noted.

"Sit your ass down before some officer has a problem with you."

Eli came over and sat down next to Vernon. "Guess my job is to watch him all day," He said as he pointed to Ray.

"You watch him and I'll watch the other," Vernon said.

Eli laughed and then remembered what it was that he wanted to tell Vernon. "My cousin wrote me a letter. I got it last week and found someone to read it to me. He's upset that there's a new law, allowing anyone who owned twenty Negroes to be discharged from the army," Eli said.

"I don't get it, why should they be allowed to go home?" Vernon asked.

"Right... Who here owns twenty slaves?" Eli asked everyone within ear shot.

"Not me," was heard from someone.

"Do you own slaves?" Eli asked a man next to him.

"No."

"Me neither," said another.

"Still don't get it," Vernon said.

"Let me spell it out for you: rich man's war, poor man's fight!"

"At least he didn't actually try to spell it," Ray said to Mike with a snicker.

"Feeling better, I see," Mike said.

"Somewhat," Ray mumbled.

"Whatta-ya think?" Mike asked Ray.

"'Bout what?" Ray asked.

"About this whole thing, dumb ass," Mike said. "How awesome is this? How many people can say they were actually at the battle of Gettysburg?"

"Oh yeah," Ray said. "This is bigger then any reenactment I've ever been in. More intense."

"Think?" Mike said.

Eli looked at the two like they were nuts and then turned his attention to Vernon. "Whatta we get paid now pards, elebmem dollars per munt?" Eli asked.

"That's if you get it. Ain't seen pay for the last six months," Vernon said.

"A lieutenant gets what, 'bout a hundred dollars a munt?" Eli said.

"Some'em like that," Vernon said.

"Does he not always get his?" Eli said.

"That's right, Eli, that's right," Vernon said slapping his knee laughing.

"Then it's only fair we get ours, right?" Eli said.

"Bring it up at the next meeting," Vernon said.

The men laughed, and as the time passed, the conversation subsided. Mike was glad he had the time to take it all in. The men were sitting in the tall green grasses in the clearing just behind the tree line of Seminary Ridge. Some lay down to catch a few winks. Ray sat quietly watching the clouds roll by.

"Seems strange that you can relax in the face of impending danger," Mike said to Ray.

First Sergeant Monroe walked up to the company. "The chaplain is here."

A man wearing the uniform of a captain walked to the front of the regiment. He wore a white collar and his shoulder straps had little crosses of gold in them. The chaplain was an older man with white hair. His face was round and he was clean shaven with the kind of smile that could make one feel at ease, even in the most dreadful of times.

"God alone controls our destinies," he began. "God alone prepares us for the things that are in store for us. There is none so wise as to foresee the future or foretell the end."

Mike and Ray exchanged looks.

"Brothers, God sometimes seems afar, but He—" The Chaplain pointed his finger skyward—"will never leave or forsake anyone who puts his trust in Him! We know that all things work and come together for those that fear God," he said with passion. "In closing, I would like to emphasize that a life given for one's country is never lost. Make your peace with God now. The power of His mercy will bring you into his arms, and unto His holy city. You will be at peace at last. Brothers, blessed you all shall be, in the Father's name, Amen." The Chaplain gave the sign of the cross and bowed his head and walked down the line to the next regiment.

Mike had never heard a sermon quite like that before. He stood up to stretch. Ray got to his feet. Eli stood in front of Ray, blocking him.

"Now what?" Ray asked.

"Care to join us men for a drink?"

"Me... are you talking to me?"

"Given the situation, yes. Look, I know ya'll are fresh fish, but it's nuthin' a little whiskey won't take care of. Besides, it's good rye whiskey."

Ray looked at Mike with a smile. "What do you think, Mike?"

"Sure, why not? Now that we're all friends," Mike said.

"Sure," Eli said.

The three sat down with Corporal Sheppard and John Vernon. Ray sat down next to Mike.

"Here's to ya," Shepard said then took a swig.

"Is this why you needed to see the sutler?" Mike asked with a smile.

"Yep, and I've been saving it for just this occasion," Corporal Sheppard said.

"What occasion?" Ray asked.

"The fight, of course. We finally get in the fight. Sure 'bout time we show them Yankee's what we's made outta. Hell, it's better than tearing up tracks all week," Vernon said.

"Yeah, bet the Cumberland Valley Railroad glad we left," Eli added.

"Guess so, but it would be safer," Ray said.

The men laughed a nervous laugh and Sheppard handed the liquor to Ray. He took a sip of the whiskey. "Holy shit, it actually vaporized in my mouth." He handed the bottle to Mike.

Mike took a drink. "Goes down smooth."

Mike handed the bottle back to Corporal Sheppard and watched as he took a long pull. "Oh, be jolly!"

Everyone laughed again, including Mike and Ray.

When Eli got the bottle, he took a long drink and swallowed. Wiping off his chin he said, "Ya know, boys, there are three essential elements to life in this world:

One's air, one's water, and one's whiskey, with whiskey being the most important of the three!"

The clock was ticking, and the soldiers began to laugh as if they didn't have a worry in the world. But Mike knew it was a release of tensions. Ray was also laughing his nervous laugh. Mike felt good. They were finally being accepted as part of the company.

Ray relaxed, "You know, Mike, Eli is not so bad after all," he said.

"All these fellows are not so bad, here's to ya," Mike said. He was enjoying the moment.

Then, all of a sudden, came two booms, one right after the other.

"They came from the direction of the peach orchard," Corporal Sheppard noted.

As the men stood up to see, the earth started to tremble with the detonation of each Confederate cannon.

Mike looked at his great grandfather's pocket watch: one o'clock. History was right on time. The cannonade for Pickett's Charge had begun.

Chapter Twenty

July 3, 1863 - Behind the Angle - 12:45 P.M.

A battery of six guns was spread out to Gordon's left with about 14 yards in between each one. Action front had already been ordered and the pieces were unlimbered. The guns were manhandled into position and the crew assumed their firing stations.

The angle was 30 yards to the front of the guns and to the right of Gordon. The copse of trees was to his left. The young Lieutenant Alonzo Cushing was in charge. Sergeant Fuger, a dashing young man of German heritage sported a van Dyke mustache and goatee and was Chief of the Peace.

Gordon's right hand was still handcuffed to the wheel of the limber. The heavy iron opened the previous wounds which started to bleed once more. The July sun beat down and there was very little air movement. Gordon began to sweat. Tugging on the handcuff only doubled the pain which was already too great.

To Gordon's surprise, his great-great-grandfather was standing next to him. He saw that his grandfather was not the sergeant major that his family always told him he was. He was just a private and had the job of lugging the ammunition from the limber to the cannon. Gordon wondered how his family had gotten it wrong.

His grandfather, with another round in his arms, walked over and stood next to the gunner. Since eleven o'clock that morning the enemy guns had been silent. The birds chirped and sang their songs.

Gordon continued to worry about his predicament. He needed a way out. He knew the cannonade would start soon. "What time is it?" Gordon finally yelled to Mortimer a few yards away. Mortimer pulled out his pocket watch and studied the hands a moment, "Three quarters past twelve," he yelled back.

"There's no time, the cannonade starts at one. You've got to get the lieutenant to set me free," Gordon pleaded. "We're family, Mort. You said so yourself."

Now curious, Mortimer walked back over. "How's that?"

"You said you have a large family. We have the same last name. Hell, we might be cousins," Gordon pointed out.

"Yeah, think so, huh?"

"Please, Mort, make him understand. I'm not a traitor or a threat. I can help him."

"Ain't my place," Mortimer said.

Gordon pleaded once more. "Please, Mort, you got to make the lieutenant understand."

"I take orders from Sergeant Fuger."

Suddenly, the ground began to tremble below their feet. Mortimer looked at Gordon and steadied his stance. Then he scurried away to the gunner. Gordon moved to the inside of the limber's wheel and crouched down.

Then, from the sky came a gale of shot and shell. An explosion above Gordon's head rained down shrapnel as the first shells of the cannonade began. Gordon realized that high tide had come.

"To your posts," Lieutenant Cushing ordered.

"With long range shot, at a distance of a thousand yards, load," the gunner yelled. The No.1 man sponged the piece and, with the weight of his body, rammed the long range shot down the barrel.

"Ready," the gunner yelled and then stepped in to make sure the gun was sighted to his satisfaction.

"Fire!" he yelled and the No.4 man gave the lanyard a good yank behind his back. The blast that followed was deafening. The cannon jumped a foot off the ground and two feet back, throwing dirt into the air. Gordon watched in shock.

"Load!" shouted the gunner. The crew manhandled the cannon back into position and loaded the gun once again. A good crew could load and fire twice a minute, but Lieutenant Cushing's orders were to keep the rate of fire to one round per minute. Gordon surmised that the lieutenant wanted to keep the generation of smoke to a minimum.

As Captain Hazard walked the line of his batteries, Brigadier General Henry Hunt, an older, but knowledgeable man with a full black beard, caught up with him.

Gordon tried to get their attention, but Hazard and Hunt didn't notice him handcuffed to the wheel just a few yards from them.

"Captain Hazard, hold your fire and let the batteries on Cemetery Hill and Little Round Top reply to the enemy's guns, understand? Wait fifteen minutes or for my orders to fire you're guns," General Hunt yelled over the noise.

"Hold your fire, lieutenant," Hazard ordered.

"Cease firing," Lieutenant Cushing ordered.

Lieutenant Milne did the same along with the other sections. The battery of six guns went silent.

Meanwhile, the Confederate cannons were roaring and belching a lead hail storm of shrapnel over Gordon's head and the rest of Captain Hazard positions. The terrified horses broke from their holders and ran.

Gordon was trying to stay low, and after a few minutes of the pounding, General Hancock rode his black stallion up the line of the Second Corps hollering, "Why are you not firing?"

He rode directly to Captain Hazard. "Captain Hazard, I want you to open fire on the enemy's position, now!"

"Sir, General Hunt said I was to wait fifteen minutes after the Confederate bombardment began before replying in order to conserve ammo for the infantry attack that is sure to follow."

Hancock glared furiously. "You'll fire now and that's an order."

Captain Hazard turned to the cannoneers. "Commence firing."

Gordon thought this might be a bad time to ask him for a favor.

The cannons roared back to life. The constant blasting of the guns was deafening. But before General Hancock could leave the area, General Hunt caught up

The Final Charge

with him. Gordon overheard the argument between General Hunt and General Hancock over the noise of exploding shells.

"You're overstepping you're authority. I am the Chief of Artillery for the entire Army of the Potomac," General Hunt yelled.

"This is my sector and that makes me in charge of everything, including your guns," Hancock yelled.

This made General Hunt visibly upset, but there was nothing he could do about it now; he warned General Hancock, "I'm going to take the matter up with General Meade after the battle."

"Go ahead, General, you have my permission."

General Hunt mumbled obscenities and walked away.

General Hancock, after getting his way, kicked his horse and rode off, shouting orders down the line as he went. When Captain Hazard saw that the general had ridden out of view, he ordered an immediate cease fire. He knew that General Hunt was right. Conserving ammunition greatly increased their chances of victory. Gordon was not only impressed with General Hunt's insubordination but was in awe that he was a witness to history.

The firing came to a stop. General Hunt looked toward Captain Hazard, smiled, and nodded his thanks.

Gordon knew why General Hunt had wanted to stop firing. Not only would it conserve ammunition, but it would help trick the Confederate commanders into believing that the Union center was weak. General Meade and General Hunt actually wanted Lee's infantry to attack.

The Confederate cannonade was still roaring, throwing its hail of deadly projectiles through the air. Gordon could hear the hissing as they passed overhead. Their guns were elevated too high and most of the shells were going over the front lines of the Federal forces behind the stone wall, but the supply train, thought to be safely out of harms way to the rear, was being decimated. Confederate shelling was destroying valuable supplies and killing most of the horses.

Fifteen minutes quickly passed and Captain Hazard ordered his battery to open fire. The gunner checked the elevation. The guns were already loaded with long range shot.

"Fire!" the gunner yelled. Fire and smoke billowed forth.

"Load!" the gunner ordered. The entire battery was quickly enveloped by smoke. The smoke generated from the muzzles of the guns finally allowed the Confederates to zone in on the enemy. They became easy targets. Gordon felt the earth tremble.

Gordon again tore at his iron shackles, ripping the skin around his wrist. He winced in pain and pleaded to anyone in earshot to un-cuff him. Mortimer was too busy lugging the shells.

Suddenly, the caisson fourteen yards to his left took a direct hit and blew up. The ammunition it held exploded in a great fire ball taking out two of Cushing's guns. It had the intensity of an earthquake. The men were torn apart. Body parts flew in the air landing at Gordon's feet. Blood and debris splashed across his face. Gordon struggled harder now, trying to break the spoke of his wheeled prison.

Another shell landed under a limber, striking the man on the opposite side. Gordon saw him hop away to the rear with one leg. The other dangled in shreds.

Lieutenant Cushing saw Gordon struggling to get free. He also noticed that he was getting in the way of the No.7 man handing the shell to the No.5 man. He took the keys from his pocket and had started to walk toward Gordon when he was hit in the shoulder by the flying debris and was knocked off his feet.

The lieutenant slowly and painfully stood up. First Sergeant Fuger came to his aid. "Steward, come quick," he shouted. But Lieutenant Cushing waved them off. "I'll be all right." He did, however, let them bandage his wound.

The gray smoke was so thick, Gordon couldn't see. A man fell to the ground in front of him. The man wrenched in pain and begged. "Shoot me, please, put me out of my agony."

Gordon recoiled in fear. He could not help him. When no one came to his aid, the man managed to pull his revolver out from its holster and he held it to his head.

Gordon watched as he pulled the trigger. Blood splattered backward leaving specks on Gordon's face.

Mortimer appeared out of the dust and smoke, jingling the keys. Gordon felt great relief seeing his grandfather come to his rescue. But before he could say thanks, another explosion occurred. A Rhode Island man who was loading his gun was hit. The gun exploded. The blast tore off the gunner's head and ripped away his left arm. The explosion also threw Mortimer to the ground screaming in pain.

"Noooo!" Gordon yelled in anguish. He felt a weird guilt come over him. He looked at Mortimer and thought: *He wouldn't have gotten hurt if it wasn't for me.*

Then he noticed the keys on the ground. He reached for the keys, stretching as far as the iron cuffs would allow. The keys were just out of reach. He tugged on his shackles even harder like an animal in a trap. He actually thought about chewing off his own arm.

Then he realized: *What if Mortimer dies? Would I even be born?* He couldn't stand the thought. Gordon then saw Lieutenant Cushing shouting orders to his men to help Mortimer.

"I can help him if you let me," Gordon shouted out of sheer desperation.

Cushing picked up the keys from the ground and walked over to Gordon. With compassion in his voice he said. "I don't like you being cuffed to the wheel any more then you do."

"I'm a... a doctor... I can save him," Gordon lied. *This day and age, a paramedic would be equivalent to a doctor,* he assumed. "Besides, I may be saving myself in the process," mumbled Gordon.

Lieutenant Cushing, seeing how defenseless he was, unlocked the irons. "I hope you can do what you say you can."

"Me too, Lieutenant," Gordon, now free, bent down to look at Mortimer. There was shrapnel in his back between his ribs. Gordon hoped that it hadn't penetrated the lung. He slowly removed the small piece of iron. Mortimer let out a painful yelp. After tearing off strips of his own shirt, Gordon used compression to stop the bleeding. Gordon bandaged the wound.

"How's your breathing?" Gordon asked.

Mortimer coughed, "Hurts."

There was no blood in his cough.

"You'll be alright, and I'll still be born."

"What?"

"I said we'll let the surgeons look at it."

The medical corps was waiting. When Gordon was done, the stewards carried Mortimer off to the rear.

"Where did you learn to do that?" Cushing asked.

"Ummm... medical school," Gordon answered with a shrug.

"Maybe you can look at mine later," Cushing said.

"Sure," Gordon answered.

"Can you carry these shells?"

"Yes, of course," Gordon replied.

"Well then, you can take his place as the No.5 man."

"I can do that," Gordon agreed.

The No.7 man handed Gordon a brown leather ammunition pouch to carry the shell. Gordon slung it over his left shoulder and went to work.

The third gun took a direct hit. The crew ran toward the rear. Cushing pulled his pistol from his holster and stopped one of the men. "The next man who leaves his post again, I'll blow his brains out."

Gordon didn't move. The men went back to their posts. For over an hour, without letup, the cannons continued to belch fire and smoke. Gordon continued to carry the ammunition as the No.5 man. The smoke and the smell of sulfur filled his nostrils until he choked. He was so caught up in the action that escape had become the last thing on his mind.

About three in the afternoon, Lieutenant Cushing echoed the order of Captain Hazard. "Cease firing," he called. All the guns in the battery went silent.

The cannonade was finally over and, as the afternoon sun got hotter, an eerie stillness came over the field. Gordon was exhausted and thirsty. His mouth was dry. He was horrified at the savagery of the whole thing. He remembered thinking back to how cool it was to read about it, to reenact it. Now he was trying to stop the uncontrollable shivering that had come over him.

Lieutenant Cushing walked over and broke him from his thoughts. "Good job."

"Thank you, sir," Gordon said.

"Well, I'm still standing, and the cannonade is over. I thought you'd foreseen my death."

"Yeah, well, I'm not always right," Gordon lied.

"Maybe the shrapnel to the shoulder is what you saw?"

"Ummm… maybe," Gordon said looking at the ground. He couldn't look him in the eye. He didn't want to tell him about his death, for fear of being put in irons again.

"The attack is about to start and I need to know, are you with us?" Cushing asked.

"Yes, sir," Gordon said as he perked up a bit. He looked out over the field. He wondered about Mike and Ray. *If they're out there, I hope my actions don't get them killed*, he thought.

Chapter Twenty-One

July 3, 1863 - Seminary Ridge - 1 P.M.
Over a hundred Confederate cannons opened fire. Mike and Ray, along with the rest of the company, were behind the tree line. They could not see the cannonade but they sure heard it, and it was deafening.

"Fall in!" ordered First Sergeant Monroe. The men grabbed their gear and formed up at the same spot where they had stacked arms. Mike grabbed Ray and over the noise of the cannon he shouted, "When we get to the fence, stop and wait."

Ray nodded.

First Sergeant Monroe yelled, "Come on, fall in where you were."

Mike and Ray hurried over and joined the ranks. Ray would have liked to stay next to Mike, but Sergeant Monroe would have none of it. He moved Ray down the line. "Here's where you were. Look familiar?" Ray knew he was supposed to be there; that's where he left his musket. Eli watched the sergeant place Ray in line. "All you have to do is look for me. Is that so hard to do?" Eli chastised.

Ray gave Eli a dumb look, "What?"

Eli straightened out his blanket roll and shook his head.

Mike was back with Vernon, who seemed to be praying. Corporal Sheppard was to Mike's right.

"Attention, brigade!" General Armistead yelled. The same was echoed by Major John C. Owens, and then echoed by each captain of the companies.

Mike heard a whistling sound. It was solid shot that passed overhead and struck the earth with a massive thud. The men ducked and covered. The Union cannons were now returning the favor.

"Take arms," was ordered by all the captains down the line. The neat stacks of rifles that looked like rows of teepees were removed and handed to their proper owner.

The cannonade was deafening. Mike's ears shut down and the explosions seemed muffled to him. Mike looked around: the flags and guidons waved quietly in the wind. Mike felt as if he was in a dream. The men didn't say much, not that they could have been heard if they did anyway.

The unpleasant odor of sulfur drifted along the rank and file. With ninety-degree heat, the stench of unwashed armpits was sickening. Added to that, there was the stale smell of whiskey breath. Mike choked from the mixture. The men looked anxious about what was to come. Ray was quiet.

After each burst, nervous whispering carried along the ranks. The men were sick with worry: they could only wait and hope they weren't next. One after another, the whoosh of solid shot passed overhead. One hit a tree, cutting it in half. There was a loud crack as it fell. Men scattered and ran and then would come slowly back to their place in line, mumbling to themselves.

"Attention, company! Quiet in the ranks," First Sergeant Roy Monroe said in a raspy voice over the noise.

Ray kept looking at the ground and wouldn't look up.

Captain Wilson turned his attention to the company and rubbed his beard with his left hand. He needed time to collect his thoughts. Then, he cracked a smile as he gazed over the men, catching each one's eye with his gaze. He stepped forward and came to attention.

The Captain's green eyes gleamed as he saw their pride. He scanned the men, sizing them up for the task ahead. He seemed to look directly at Ray when he said:

"You will obey orders. Do not anticipate them. Listen to your officers and you will stand a much better chance of coming out of this alive. Do your duty and make us proud."

Mike got a strange feeling of awe from the captain's words. He looked around at the men. He thought they would be more scared, but for some reason, all the pent-up nervousness that had built up all that day was somehow gone. The men had gone from being scared sick out of their mind to feeling mean. The soldiers became jubilant and certain of success. Mike could see the return of self-confidence in the features of the soldiers beside him. Vernon was smiling ear to ear. They were going to whip the whole Yankee army this time for sure.

Mike felt a sense of wonder as he stood there. *Only human beings can look directly into the face of death, knowing there's a good chance they'll all get killed, and say, 'We can do it.'*

Pickett's Division was at the tree-line on the west side of Seminary Ridge. There they were out of sight of the Union lines. Mike remembered that the divisions of General Trimble and General Pettigrew were also forming along the same ridge to the north.

Mike watched General Armistead silently standing there waiting for General Garnett's brigade, which was to his front, to step off. When the last company of that brigade started to move, the moment had come. The field music began to play. General Armistead smiled and ordered, "Brigade, forward, march!"

Mike experienced an eerie feeling as the brigade moved into the woods. The companies moved through the thickets and undergrowth of the woods. A tree branch hit Ray in the face when the soldier in front pulled the branch back and let it fly.

They marched and yelled obscenities. Ray was in his glory. They stepped on thorny bushes and cussed some more. The snapping of branches was heard as the men broke dead tree limbs. They came out on the other side of the woods and were halted. Ray very gingerly pulled off a sticker bush branch from his face.

Here, at the edge, Mike saw the Confederate artillery commander, Colonel E. Porter Alexander; he looked just like the photographs. Mike gave a slight smile as he watched the Confederate artillerist direct the bombardment of the federal position on Cemetery Ridge. *I want so bad to yell, the fuses are cut to long, but what good would it do.*

Under cover of the trees they waited for the cannonade to stop. The Confederates were getting the worst of the artillery duel. Federal shells were decimating the infantry waiting in the woods behind the Confederate Artillery line.

"Jesus, if the solid shot doesn't get ya, the trees would get cut in half, fall, and kill ya," Mike said.

Every now and then a gun or a sword would fly through the air and sometimes hit another man who would cry out in agony. Ray's face got speckled with blood as human appendages went flying past him. He went pale with fear. *If they're getting killed here, what will happen when we march out?* Ray thought.

Mike leaned forward and looked down the rank at Ray. "You okay down there?"

"Yeah, I'm all right," Ray lied.

Eli, who was next to Ray, leaned over. "I'll take good care of 'em fer ya," he said.

Mike went back into position. He looked at Corporal Sheppard, who had the look of both despair and excitement on his gray face as he waited for the inevitable.

The Confederate artillery went silent. Mike realized that the federal artillery shelling had also stopped. Everything went eerily quiet. The next sound Mike heard, other then the ringing in his head, was officer's sabers clanging as they moved about the lines.

There were heavy footfalls and pants ruffling as the guides ran to their positions. It was about two-thirty in the afternoon and Pickett's Charge was about to begin.

Chapter Twenty-Two

July 3, 1863 - The Angle - 2:30 P.M.
Gordon leaned on the rock wall, swatting at the flies with Lieutenant Cushing. They were looking out across the farmer's field in the direction of Seminary Ridge.

"Damn horse flies," Cushing said as he smashed one against the rock.

Gordon reflected on the stone wall, how it was originally built by farmers placing field stones they unearthed when they plowed their land to divide their property lines. Now, it was built up a little stronger and being used as breastworks for the Union Army.

Gordon looked to his left and saw the copse of trees that would become known as the High Water Mark of the Confederacy. It was the center of the Union's line where Lee would focus his attack. He also knew that General Meade's headquarters was to the rear of his location. Just over the hill behind Cemetery Ridge.

Gordon was beginning to like First Lieutenant Alonzo Cushing, the dashing 22-year old with brown eyes and dark hair who had been wounded in the shoulder during the cannonade but stayed in the action and refused to leave the field. Gordon remembered reading that he was driven by duty, but to witness it firsthand was something else.

"Hey Lon," Second Lieutenant Joseph A. Milne called walking over to him. "What ya'll looking at?"

"Nothing, at the moment," Cushing said.

"How's your shoulder?" Milne asked.

"Still hurts, but I've been trying to ignore it."

Milne was even younger than Cushing and one of the few men here with no facial hair. Gordon thought he looked sort of like a politician. He was in charge of the gun next to Cushing, only fourteen yards away.

Gordon worried about his great-great-grandfather who had also been wounded during the cannonade, and was taken off the field by stretcher.

"Lieutenant, may I ask a question?"

"Go 'head," Cushing said.

"Where did they take my grand—I mean, my cousin?"

"Far as I know, all the wounded were taken to the 11th Corps field hospital beyond that hill," he pointed to Cemetery Hill.

"Thanks, Lieutenant," Gordon said.

"You seem to know what you're doing. Think you can take a look at my injury?"

"Sure thing, Lieutenant."

Gordon unwrapped the bloody bandages that the steward had placed on the wound. He saw a two-inch gash where shrapnel had laid open his skin to the bone. There was clothing and dirt in the wound but, not wanting to worry the lieutenant, Gordon said, "Looks good, but I'd like to change the bandages, if that's okay."

"Steward, another bandage," Cushing yelled.

The steward ran over and handed the lieutenant a clean bandage. Cushing handed it to Gordon.

"Thanks," Gordon said as he removed the old bandages. "Anybody have any whiskey?"

"Devil water," Lieutenant Milne said.

"Will this do?" The steward pulled a flask from his own coat pocket.

"That'll work," Gordon said. He poured some whiskey on Cushing's wound making him flinch and pull away.

"What the hell you doing, is this payback for me handcuffing you to the wheel?"

"Of course not Lieutenant; I'm killing germs."

"Killing what?"

"Nothing, I'm just cleaning the wound." Gordon's slip of the tongue made sweat develop on his forehead. He placed a clean bandage over the wound.

"There, that ought to do it."

"Thanks, I think," Cushing said. "You should be working at the field hospital, not here lugging shells."

Before Gordon could say anything, First Sergeant Frederick Fuger walked over. "Lieutenant Lon, can I join ya, sir?"

"Sure, grab a seat," Cushing said.

"What's that?" A gunner yelled. "Come here, look at this!"

Gordon stood with the rest and looked out across the farmer's field toward Seminary Ridge. They saw a glimmering light coming from the woods. The light ran the length of the woods.

"There, I see it," said Cushing.

"What is it?" Milne asked.

"My God," Gordon whispered. For a moment, he was the only one who knew what it was.

The light broke up into thousands of smaller lights. Gordon let out a sigh; coming out of the woods was the Confederate infantry. The lights were their bayonets reflecting in the sunlight. It was close to three and they were preparing for the assault.

Cushing saw the Confederates begin to assemble along the tree line, forming their columns. "To your posts," Cushing ordered. "It's time for paybacks."

Gordon and the rest of the men ran the thirty yards back to their guns and took their positions.

"Load with long range shot," Cushing told the gunner.

"Load," the gunner ordered. He aimed his cannon and stepped back in position. "Ready! Fire!"

When the shot reached its target on the ridge, the rebel officers and men scattered as a plume of dirt and debris rose into the air.

Cushing's cannoneers cheered. Gordon hoped that if Mike and Ray were out there, the shot hadn't killed them.

Cushing didn't notice Captain Hazard standing right behind him and looked to be annoyed. The ammunition was already in short supply. When the cheering died down Captain Hazard yelled, "Young man, are you aware that every round you fire costs the government two dollars and sixty-seven cents?"

"Yes, sir. Sorry, sir. Won't happen again, sir," Lieutenant Cushing said and winked at Gordon.

Gordon knew the Confederates were about to make their historic final charge in a matter of minutes. He also knew how the charge would end. But now he started to have doubts about it. *What if it's different this time?*

Chapter Twenty-Three

July 3, 1863 - Seminary Ridge - 2:30 P.M.
As the men formed their battle front, a well-placed shell exploded, up-heaving the earth. Mike ducked for cover as the men and officers scattered. The shot just missed them. After a few minutes, they cautiously walked back and reformed their lines.

Major John C. Owens stepped to the regiment's front. "Attention, battalion. Attention to orders. Hold your fire until we reach Emmitsburg Road. The enemy will not be in range until then anyway. I do not want to hear the rebel yell until then, either."

There was excitement down the ranks. Mike and Ray watched in amazement as General Pickett, the flamboyant, high-spirited Virginian came riding into view. He wore his best dress uniform and looked dapper upon his milk-white horse.

He rode along the front ranks reviewing his men. Mike thought he could smell Pickett's perfume as he came to a halt and stood in his stirrups. Pickett raised his sword and shouted, "Up, men, and to your posts! Don't forget today that you are from Old Virginia!" Cheering broke out throughout the ranks. The ground shook with the cheers. Some men started to cry with pride.

The General's morale-boosting words gave the soldiers a sort of halo, illuminating every face. His presence reinforced the feeling of victory and success. Ray held back tears that formed in his eyes. He didn't understand until now, this very moment, what reenactors felt in their hearts and the deep respect they had for their ancestors.

Mike, also misty eyed, was coming to grips with the event.

Major Owens yelled, "Attention, battalion! Forward! Guide center! Marrrch!"

It was three o'clock, and Pickett's charge had begun.

Captain Wilson echoed the major's orders for his company, while Sergeant Monroe began yelling orders of his own. "Dress right! Come on, dress it up! Dress to the colors!"

The drum-and-fife started to play as Pickett's division left the cover of the trees. The Confederate battle flags and guidons flapped in the breeze as the men advanced, passing through Colonel Alexander's cannons. The rank and file were tight and kept a synchronized step. Officers' sabers, tin cups, and canteens clanked as rank after rank of soldiers pressed forward through the tall grass. The army had started its mile-long march toward the clump of trees in the center of the federal lines.

As the last rank moved past Colonel Alexander's guns and into the knee-high grass, federal artillery resumed firing. The ground began to shake.

"Shit, that's close," Eli said.

Shock waves cracked the sky as the timed shells exploded above their heads. Men began to fall in the first seven minutes, passing over only a quarter mile.

Over the repeated detonations, Sergeant Monroe yelled as loud as he could, "Promptly, men, close it up. The guide is to the colors!"

John Vernon twisted his ankle and fell, letting out a sharp howl of pain. He pulled on Mike's coat as he went down. Mike stopped to help, "You hit?"

"I'm okay, damn gopher hole," he said.

"Get up," Mike encouraged.

With a little help from Mike, Vernon got to his feet and kept going. All around them, men were being killed by shrapnel. Blood splattered on Mike's face. The nice straight lines came apart and then came back together again because of the uneven topography. The wounded and dying began to litter the field.

As men fell, puddles formed on the field from where they bled out. Mike and Ray closed up the rank and moved toward each other. At first, Mike tried to avoid stepping into the blood but, after awhile, fatigue set in and it didn't seem to matter anymore; his brogans became caked with blood and dirt.

Ray was leaning close to Eli for protection. Vernon was still beside Mike. They had to step over the dead and around the dying as they moaned and begged for water. Mike wanted to stop and help them, but Corporal Sheppard kept the men moving forward.

"No time to help them now," Corporal Sheppard shouted over the noise. He wanted it to be perfectly clear: They had to keep moving.

In fourteen minutes, they were halfway across the field. Armistead's brigade was still behind Garnett's brigade and Kemper's to the right-front.

Large gaps in the lines opened when as many as ten men at a time fell because of flying hot iron from the bursting of a single shell. Soldiers in the rear constantly moved up to fill the gaps in the ranks that were made by the shrapnel. Mike and Ray finally came together. Eli and Vernon were right beside them. They all followed Corporal Sheppard who was following Captain Wilson.

Gray smoke from cannon fire that Mike used to love so much at reenactments rolled over the field. It blackened his face and at times obscured his vision making it hard to see where he was going.

Ray choked from the smoke and dust that was thrown up from the ground. He cursed and wished it would all stop.

"Come on, we're almost there," Mike said.

"Dress it up," Sergeant Monroe yelled.

Twenty minutes had passed. The confederates had crossed over three quarters of the field. The fence that lined Emmitsburg Road was in sight. The cadence quickened and the orders came more rapidly and were only given once.

They were tight-faced warriors with unwavering bravery. They walked into the savagery with their heads angled down as though it were raining.

The color-bearers proudly waved their flags as they lead the brigades. The officers moved back and forth from front rank to rear rank, keeping the alignment as best they could.

"Battalion! Left Oblique! March! Guide center! Guide on the colors!" Major Owens yelled.

The change in direction was an attempt to elude the enemy, but the federal guns were now pointed directly at the flanks of the brigade. The Confederate infantry was being enfiladed. The firing came from the right, the Union guns on Little Round Top as well as Cemetery Ridge.

The Confederate armies were stretched out for over a mile. The divisions of Pettigrew and Trimble converged on Armistead's division. They intermixed, forming a single large force for the final assault against the Union center. Mike and Ray were crowded by the other regiments, which slowed their forward progress.

Mike noticed Ray looking to his right, into the distance. From the direction of Cemetery Ridge, he could see neat donut-hole spirals coming from the cannons when they fired. At that moment, Mike remembered reading that the forty-five-degree oblique march gave the Union guns a straight shot down the Confederate ranks.

Ray was staring at them when Mike jerked him to the ground. Ray hit the earth with a thud. "Why'd you do that?" But before Ray got his answer, the shock wave struck. It seemed that the hot flames of hell were turned loose above them. Mike heard the Union shells whirling through the air just over their heads. Ray tried to get up to take a look.

Mike saw a bellow of smoke leave the Union cannons. "Keep your head down, Ray! Here it comes again."

Chapter Twenty-Four

July 3, 1863 - Union Front Lines - 2:30 P.M.

Gordon saw skirmishers advancing into the farmer's field. Within minutes, the entire Confederate attacking force was in view. *It's started,* he thought, *Pickett's Charge has started.*

The Confederate lines were formed with precision as they came on. Flags and banners waved in the sultry air.

"What a sight," the gunner said, seemingly with admiration.

"Memorable," Milne whispered.

Such strange feelings, Gordon thought as he stood next to them and looked across the field. For the first time in his life, felt the magnitude of it. It looked like the whole Confederate army was coming his way. Gordon noticed that there were no flies or birds in the air. *Even the birds knew when to leave,* he thought.

Gordon saw the officers on horseback galloping up and down their ranks. He could only imagine the fortitude it must have taken to cross that mile-long field.

In seven minutes, the Confederate army was a quarter mile across the field. Over the cannon blasting, Gordon, at times, could hear the distant sounds of men on the march with their flags flapping in the wind and the fife and drums playing.

Now and then, Gordon heard the horses' whinnies and snorts. He could hear the clanking of bit and bridle.

As they got closer, Gordon heard the officers yelling orders that he could not make out.

Gordon's eyes wandered the field and came to rest on the double fence lining Emmitsburg Road. It looked like a distance of about two hundred yards from where he was.

He remembered from reading his maps that there was a hollow before the fence and another at his immediate front.

"Must be about fifteen-thousand men," Milne said.

"More like twelve-thousand," Gordon said.

"What do you know?" Milne said sharply.

"Sorry, Lieutenant," Gordon said, realizing his argument was worthless and may only lead to more trouble that he didn't need.

"I know one thing for sure. It stretches as far as the eye can see," Cushing said.

They were standing at the front of the cannon when Captain Hazard, commander of the artillery, walked up to the men. "To your posts!" He ordered.

The men quickly assumed their firing stations. Since the long range shot was in short supply, Hazard knew he needed to conserve.

"Load, but wait until they're within range," Hazard ordered Lieutenant Cushing.

Gordon was at the limber as a No.5 man and was handed the next shell to be loaded. He went to the front of the cannon and stood next to the No.2 man.

"With long range shell, fuse cut at seven-hundred yards, load," the gunner ordered.

Gordon handed the shell to the No.2 man who pushed the round into the muzzle of the gun. The No.1 man rammed it down the barrel.

"Ready," the gunners ordered. The No.3 man, the vent keeper, removed the thumb stall, and with the priming wire, poked the charge and placed the friction primer into the vent.

The No.4 man hooked the lanyard to the primer. The No.3 man held it so that the No.4 man could stretch it out behind his back.

Meanwhile, Gordon watched the Confederates advance: it was the hottest part of the day. The rebel lines seemed to move slowly, but the sounds of brogans grew louder.

"Wait for it," Sergeant Fuger calmly said with a slight German accent.

The cannons on Little Round Top to Gordon's left, and Cemetery Hill to his right, had already opened fire on the advancing rebels with their long-range shot and shell. Gordon watched as spirals of gray smoke followed the solid shot out of the guns. Sweat flowed from his forehead as he watched men fall.

Gordon noticed Major General Winfield Scott Hancock, the 39-year-old commander of the Second Army Corps sitting superbly upon his black stallion. He seemed very calm as the battle started, as if on review. He held the Second Corps from firing and made no attempt to check the advance of the enemy: He wanted to conserve ammunition.

Gordon had read where Brigadier General Henry J. Hunt, Second Army Corps Artillery Chief, agreed to hold their fire until the first Confederate battalion had arrived within range of the Union position, at which point he would open fire. The Confederate forces steadily marched on.

"What a sight to behold," Cushing said.

They were watching in awe, and waiting. For Gordon, the waiting was the worst. He hated the feeling of anticipation.

Gordon scanned the field, analyzing the situation. He marveled that the front rank men had their bayonets pointed toward the front and that the rear rank men had their bayonets pointed toward the sky at right shoulder shift. He imagined, as in a dream, the sunlight dancing along the rows of bayonets, putting on a show.

Gordon watched the volleys of shot and shell exploding above the rebel lines, blowing large holes into the Confederate ranks. He snapped out of his trance when he saw body parts being thrown into the air.

Gordon stared with tears forming in his eyes as the reality of it set in. Gray and butternut passed over half the valley.

Gordon looked around at his own crew and saw their tight faces. He could feel their tenseness and anticipation of what was to come. He started to think about his own predicament. *How did I get here? How do I get home?* And then he said aloud: "What if I'm stuck here for the rest of my life?" The gunner overheard him. "At this rate, the rest of your life is not long."

Gordon looked up at the heavens and saw that the skies here were clear and blue. "Lord, give me strength," he prayed.

The Union commanders at the angle still waited for the Confederates to get in range before they dared expend one round of the precious ammunition that remained on hand.

General Hancock rode up and down the lines upon his black stallion. When he saw that the Confederates were within range, he finally reared up his war horse and came to a stop at Battery A, pointing at Lieutenant Cushing. "Commence firing."

Chapter Twenty-Five

July 3, 1863 - The Emmitsburg Road - 2:53 P.M.
The detonation and shock wave that rolled over Mike and Ray was horrific. It felt like an earthquake. Mike rose and shook off a dizzy sensation. He watched as men passed by him. He pulled Ray to his feet. "You okay?"

Ray tried to brush the dirt off his shirt and then realized it was pieces of human flesh and blood. He looked at Mike for answers that no one would have.

Corporal Sheppard tapped Mike's shoulder. "Gotta go."

Mike motioned that he understood. "Stay in control, Ray, suppress your panic," Mike yelled.

Vernon came up beside Mike, walking without help.

"How's the ankle?" Mike asked.

"Better," Vernon said.

"Have you seen Eli?" Ray asked.

"For all I know, you're wearing him," Mike said.

Mike led Ray along by the arm through the smoke and the uneven terrain. Ray struggled to pull his mind back from the shock. He stumbled over the bodies of the fallen.

"Watch where you're going," Ray yelled. "You're dragging me." Mike let go of his arm and Ray dropped to one knee. He recoiled sharply as his knee came down on something soft. He looked down and saw that he had knelt on a severed forearm.

"Christ, Mike, I'm tripping over body parts."

"Can't help that," Mike said.

They rejoined their company, and as more explosions occurred they filled in the ranks. The sky rained hot metal down on them. The heat was oppressing. Dense smoke drifted along the ground. The stench of sulfur filled their nostrils as they tried to breathe. The dust stung their eyes. The men coughed constantly.

Through the breaks in the drifting smoke, Mike glimpsed the fence line at Emmitsburg Road; it looked to be about forty yards ahead. Garnett and Kemper's brigades were still to the front-right of Armistead.

"Dress it up, men!" ordered Major Owens.

Captain Wilson echoed the orders over the booming so that the men would hear. One company after another adjusted to the battalion's forward movement. Mike and Ray were pushed in whatever direction the company took. As the men fell, Mike had to constantly move to the right, dressing the ranks. With every regiment doing the same, it slowed the forward movement of the whole division.

The regiment finally came to a shallow swale ten yards from the fence line just before Emmitsburg Road. First Sergeant Monroe saw that it could provide partial cover to his company. "Here, boys, we'll regroup here."

As the shells exploded overhead, Monroe stood on the crest waving his arms. He tried desperately to get his men into the depression.

Mike saw him. "There, Ray, that's where we need to be."

Sergeant Monroe suddenly twisted completely around to his rear and fell into the swale. Mike was paralyzed at the sight. He stopped and stared at the First Sergeant; the way he was twisted and mangled, he had to be dead. The carnage was now getting to Mike.

More gaps appeared in the lines as Mike watched a first lieutenant also reach the crest. "Close it up men! Close it up!"

Another shell exploded above them. The lieutenant bent over in agony when a large piece of hot iron disemboweled him. Mike saw abdominal viscera roll out into the dirt where the lieutenant fell.

Mike had enough; something in his mind snapped. He ran and took the lieutenant's place on the depression. "Here men, take cover here." As the projectiles whizzed by, Mike hurried Ray into the natural trench.

Captain Wilson, seeing Mike, followed his example and got into the hollow. More men piled into the small area, each soldier making room for another. They hugged the ground with their faces to the dirt. John Vernon got in followed by Eli Corbit. Corporal Leon Sheppard got in and, staying as low as possible, said to Mike, "I think you just earned stripes."

Ray looked at Eli and then at his own jacket, still stained with blood. "Wasn't you."

Soon the whole division was bogged down at the fence line while Union artillery constantly shelled them.

Mike's heart sank; something was wrong. There was not just one post and rail fence lining the road, but two: They lined both sides of the road. "Damn, didn't think of that," Mike mumbled.

There was no more room in the depression and the regiment's forward movement was halted. Captain Wilson stood up and tried to rally his men. "To the fence," he ordered. The captain ran to the fence, but very few men followed. No one wanted to move out of the only protection they had. Mike looked around. The few that did follow the captain were cut down.

Witnessing this, Mike felt a strange obligation rise within him. He could hear metal hit flesh. Men were being killed, but for some, their fate was worse than death. The mortal wounds they received didn't kill them instantly. They had to lie there and suffer. Mike heard their gut-wrenching cries for help and their hopeless moaning when help didn't come.

In the depression, the men were pushing their dead comrades' bodies sideways like sandbags to protect themselves. The shelling continued to decimate those at the fence line.

Mike felt that the groans of the wounded were worse than the thunder of battle.

Through breaks in the smoke, he saw the barn. *All I have to do is get to the barn and go home. So close.* Then he looked at the fence and the captain, to whom he now felt a commitment. Escaping to the barn was no longer an option. He stood up. "Ray, stay here," he said, and left the protection of the swale. "To the fence, men," he hollered as he ran toward the fence.

"What about the plan?" Ray yelled.

The Final Charge

Some men stood up and ran with Mike to join their captain. The men tried to climb over the fence at first, but were cut to pieces. One by one, the bodies began to pile up along the fence line. Mike got beside Captain Wilson and started to push on the rails.

Ray, still in the swale, saw Mike and the captain's bravery. He buried his face in the dirt. After a while, he knew he couldn't just stay there. He realized he couldn't go home without Mike. Finding his courage, Ray stood up and left the protection of the small trench and ran. He joined Mike. "What happened to, 'wait at the fence'?"

Mike didn't answer as he was too busy helping push the fence down with the other soldiers. Ray felt a presence and looked over his shoulder to his left and saw Eli. Ray acknowledged him with a nod. Corporal Shepard and John Vernon made it to the fence, followed by the rest of the brigade. The Union shelling hit the fence all around them as they pushed.

With tears swelling in his eyes, Ray worked harder than he ever had before. Finally, with one good push, the fence rails came down and the butternut and gray line started to move.

They crossed over Emmittburg Road to the second fence. Union shelling had blown holes in the fence and weakened what remained. The line's momentum made the second fence come down a lot quicker.

"At the double quick, marrrch!" Major Owens shouted. Captain Wilson echoed the order as he started to run the last 200 yards.

Chapter Twenty-Six

July 3, 1863 - The Angle - 3:11 P.M.
When the first rebel columns reached the fence line at Emmitsburg Road, they were within range for canister.

The guns of the 4th U.S. Artillery opened fire. Lieutenant Cushing was firing one round per minute to conserve his ammunition until the enemy got closer.

Cushing felt that General Webb's Pennsylvanians were vulnerable at the stone wall. It seemed to him they needed more fire power. "You men there, of the 71st, I need some of you over here," he yelled.

Several men came over and joined what remained of Cushing's crew.

"To the front," Cushing ordered. He made his orders clearer: "To the wall."

The gun crew and men of the 71st groaned as they pushed two of Cushing's guns down to the stone wall. Gordon was right behind them carrying as many canister rounds as he could.

When they got to the wall, the men of the 69th made room for them. The gun was loaded, and the gunner yelled, "Fire!" But before two privates from the 71st could get out of the way, the gun went off.

They had no time to react to the tragedy. The rebels were tearing down the fence. Cushing ordered the firing rate now at three per minute. The noise the cannon made was deafening. The temperature must have been ninety degrees and the humidity was stifling. Gordon took a moment and wiped his brow and he heard a cracking sound. He looked out toward the fences that lined the road. They were coming down. The Confederates were on the move again and fast approaching.

With his slight German accent, Sergeant Fuger said, "Here they come."

Just as in the history books, I'm looking at the elephant, Gordon thought. The Confederates now moved within musketry range.

The rumbling of the Confederate brigades with their flags waving was daunting, but impressive.

"Steady men. Hold your fire," General Webb said to the 69th and 71st Pennsylvania at the wall. Gordon knew he was waiting until the rebels were within optimum striking distance to deliver his deadly volley.

Cushing was still shooting canister into their ranks. When the Rebels moved within 100 yards of the Union forces, the leading columns seemed to disappear. Gordon knew they were in a depression.

Gordon watched. Cushing watched. General Webb watched from his saddle.

Then two Union regiments to the left of Gordon wheeled out of line and opened with an oblique fire upon the right of the enemy's column in the swale.

***

Deafening musketry erupted from the Union's left. Mike could see the regiments in front of him were being flanked by a federal infantry column. A second Lieutenant screamed. "Dress it up promptly, steady men, at the double-quick, marrrch!"

The regiment left the swale, following the lieutenant. He waved his sword like a madman and screamed, "Home, boys, home! Remember, home is over beyond those hills!"

***

Seemingly out of nowhere, it looked as if the rebels came out of the ground not more then twenty yards away. It was as if the whole Confederate army was coming Webb's way and fast.

Musket balls flew from every direction. They whizzed by, followed by the thump when hitting the flesh of the men firing the two three-inch ordinance guns that Cushing had pushed to the rock wall.

Cushing's No.3 man was killed, leaving only himself to be his own vent stopper. He did not have a leather thumb stall to protect his hand from the hot barrel. He brought forth his courage and secured the vent with his bare thumb.

Gordon's head felt vertigo, but he managed to hand off the next round to the gunner who placed it in the muzzle and rammed it down the bore while the lieutenant plugged the vent.

The guns were reloaded and fired one round after another. It wasn't long before Cushing's thumb was burned to the bone from the hot gun. Cushing saw Webb watching from his horse. "I will give them one more shot, sir."

They were in the process of loading the two guns when suddenly Cushing was hit in the groin by a flying piece of hot iron. He fell against the gun and slid to the ground, holding his wound. He looked down and saw his gut protruding. First Sergeant Fredrick Fuger rushed to his side. "Lon, are you okay?"

Sergeant Fuger, seeing the lieutenant's gut bulging out, called for the medical stewards to bring a stretcher.

Gordon dropped the next canister on the ground and went to his side. When the stewards got there Cushing waved them away. Fuger begged the Lieutenant to leave the field with the stewards and get medical attention. Gordon felt helpless. He knew this was how it had to be.

"Help me up," Cushing said. Fuger and Gordon helped him stand.

"Please, Lon," Fuger begged. But Cushing refused. He waved them off with his hand. Instead, while holding in his own guts, he gave the order to Fuger to fire. "Fred, give them double canister," Cushing whispered.

"Let 'em have it!" Sergeant Fuger shouted as he held up Cushing. But the gunner was killed before he could get the shot off. Bayonets and rifle butts clanged as the Confederates approached the wall. Gordon, stunned, backed away. *What was Webb waiting for?*

"Fire the damn -"

At that very moment, a minie' ball entered Cushing's open mouth and blew out the back of his head as he tried to shout the order. He fell from the arms of the sergeant to the ground, dead.

Ignoring his own safety, Gordon took the gunner's place and grabbed the lanyard from his dead fingers.

At the same time, Sergeant Fuger, tight jawed and with fire in his eyes, grabbed the first gun's lanyard. With tears in their eyes and the Confederates coming over the wall, in perfect unison, he and Gordon gave the lanyards a good yank. The resulting discharge was total devastation for the confederate men. Two fifty-foot-wide gaps opened up in the Confederate line.

***

Mike and Ray, along with their regiment, made it to the second swell. Garnett and Kemper's brigades pushed forward toward the angle. The battlefield was engulfed in a dense cloud of black smoke and debris. Chilling screams rose out of the blackness and into the air until the air, itself, became alive.

***

Gordon watched as more Confederates arrived within ten yards of the stone wall. General Webb finally greeted them. "Rise up! Fire by company—Commence firing!"

It was deadly; rows of men went down. The Confederate's nice, straight lines were decimated. It seemed to Gordon that the withering fire from both musket and cannon melted the enemy lines away. He felt a wave of nausea from the sight of it.

Gordon watched as solid shot struck the knapsack of a walking Confederate soldier, cutting it open and sending its contents flying in all directions. The man was knocked to the ground—the knapsack had saved his life—but got up a few moments later, only to be shot down again.

But the Confederates kept up the fire, more Union artillery men around Gordon began to fall. The No.2 man fell first, followed by the No.1 man. The smoke from the black powder began to burn Gordon's eyes. His mouth was full of dirt, making him spit and cough. His ears were ringing constantly.

***

Mike watched as Garnett's men were taking a beating at the stone wall. The Union men poured deadly fire down on them. There were only ten yards separating enemy from enemy; the fighting became a contest of who could tear a cartridge and ram it down the barrel faster then their foe. Volley after volley of the deadly hot lead was poured into the rank and file of both sides. The barrels of the muskets became too hot to handle. Some men poured water from their canteens onto the barrels to cool them down.

The forward brigades were bogged down just outside the stone wall. General Armistead was waving his black slouch hat from the tip of his sword shouting, "Come on boys, give them the cold steel! Who will follow me?"

Armistead's brigade rushed forward passing through the brigades of Garnett and Kemper. The ninth Virginia regiment was headed for the wall, right where Cushing's battery was located, just behind the angle.

Now, Mike could hear the officers of both the blue and the gray yelling their orders. Mike couldn't make out whose orders he was to listen to.

***

And then Gordon heard it for the first time. One by one, the scream started an awesome, fearful sound. Slowly, it grew louder and louder until it was heard by all. Armistead leaped over the rock wall followed by officers and men with the spine-tingling shrill of the Rebel Yell. They were demons from hell and they were coming to destroy the Yankee army.

Gordon saw the rebel devils coming and it seemed to him that no matter what they threw at them, they would keep coming.

***

With fixed bayonets, the rebels charged, Mike and Ray among them, screaming their heads off. Mike noticed that there was a cannon pointed straight at them. He pulled Ray backwards to the ground, knocking the air out of him. Suddenly, there was a swishing sound over Mike's head; a double canister just missed them.

"You okay?" Mike yelled to Ray.

"Yeah," Ray said.

Mike saw that the man next to him was hit. He first saw his brown hair then recognized the little patch of hair under his lower lip. It had to be John Vernon, who now laid there with his wound spurting blood in his last moments before death. Mike was livid.

Ray laid there a moment, his head tilted backwards, and his mouth agape. He tried to get up, but couldn't. He fumbled with his words. "Hel-Help me up."

Mike pulled him to his feet.

"Let's go," Ray said with a renewed strength and determination. Mike heard the anger in his voice.

It didn't matter any more that the musket balls were whirling by from every direction. Mike ignored the danger. As the flesh was being torn from the men around him, Mike was on a new mission: He wanted to kill all the Yankees. He wanted to stop this lunacy.

Mike was out for blood. He could smell it. He could taste it. He and Ray—who was also caught up in the mayhem—ran to the stone wall.

Chapter Twenty-Seven

July 3, 1863 - The Angle - 3:30 P.M.
Gordon watched the Confederates hit the stone wall right where General Webb's brigade was posted. Webb's men gave them one last volley. But when they saw the fury in the rebels' eyes, they abandoned their positions and ran away.

The rebels seemed emboldened by this indication of weakness and pushed forward with unrelenting force. Gordon was shocked to see the Confederates cross the breastwork abandoned by Webb's men. The reality of battle was surreal. The books told of it, even explained it, but to experience it firsthand was complete and utter revulsion.

***

The neat, long lines that made up the Confederate grand army were now gone. They had been replaced by a mob. Battle flags dropped to the ground only to be picked up a second later to keep the gray line moving while under heavy federal fire.

Mike and Ray jumped over the dead to climb over the stone wall. Mike looked around and saw a Union general on a dark-brown horse yelling at his men to fire at the Virginians coming over the wall.

***

Gordon watched the rebel battle flags waving over the stone wall as the rebels came over it. The Confederates had gained a foothold.

Was history changed? Were the Confederates going to win this time? He tried to collect his thoughts as his battery was about to be overrun.

***

Mike and Ray were now fighting for their very existence inside the angle as savage hand-to-hand combat ensued. The same Union general with his legs straight out in his stirrups was still yelling from his war horse, "Keep up the fire. Pour it into them!"

Mike wanted to take a shot at him, but had no time to reload. There were two Union men in his face. In his fury, he swung the rifle like a bat and fought anyone who came near him.

Ray watched in horror as Eli Corbit, along with several other men, got the full effect of double canister. Eli let out a horrific shriek as he fell to the ground: He had been torn in half. "*Eli!*" Ray screamed.

Mike took Ray by the arm. "Come on," he said. "They're retreating."

The Yankees were on the run and the Confederate battle flags were raised above the ground. They had taken Cemetery Hill.

Ray stopped to reload while Mike ran ahead. Two fleeing Yankees turned toward Mike and took a knee. They leveled their muskets and were about to fire. Mike turned his musket sideways, held it out front of him, and charged the two men. He crashed headlong into the two, knocking them backwards to the ground. Their muskets discharged into the air.

Mike was up first and used the butt of his rifle to strike both men down. For Mike, anyone in a blue uniform was fair game. It was now a mob brawl. Each man became his own general.

***

Gordon saw the rebels coming his way and without anyone left to stop them, they had a clear path to Cushing's Battery. They were immediately overrun by the 9th Virginia regiment led by General Armistead.

One attacking rebel went completely crazy, jumped on the cannon, and waved his hat like he was riding a horse. With fire in his eyes, he looked like a madman. He made an easy target for the Yankees and was immediately riddled with lead.

Armistead was shot and fell to the ground. He leaned against the wheel of Cushing's gun. Sergeant Fuger saw that the general had fallen and went to his aid. Armistead gave the Masonic sign for help. A Union captain recognized its meaning and joined Sergeant Fuger at his side. They both knelt down beside General Armistead to comfort him. Fuger gave him a drink of water from his canteen. Meanwhile, all seemed lost for the Union, as the enemy rushed on.

***

Mike saw the Union general sitting upon his war horse trying to rally his troops. Mike looked at the situation and knew that the joyous moment of victory was about to end. But to his pleasant surprise he witnessed the following.

"Charrrge!" The Union general ordered his men, but they did not.

"Fix bayonets!" He ordered. They did nothing.

"Charrrge! Damn it!" He screamed. And again they did nothing.

The general, while still on his horse, leaned down from his saddle and tried to seize the regimental flag, but the bearer would not yield it. The two wrestled over it until, in utter disgust, he rode toward the clump of trees.

***

Gordon spun around hearing the same general yell "Charrrge!" but no one moved. Gordon recognized him as General Webb. *Did they not recognize him?*

Gordon turned and focused his attention on a colonel who had stopped General Hancock. "Sir, Colonel Arthur Devereux of the 19th Massachusetts. General, they have broken through. The colors are coming over the stone wall. Let me go in there."

"Go in there pretty God-damned quick!" Snapped General Hancock from his black charger.

Gordon watched in horror as General Hancock was shot from his horse. In his bewilderment, he felt a primal rage rise within him.

***

A moment earlier, Mike had leveled his rifle-musket at General Hancock's head and pulled the trigger. *Click-boom* and the general fell from his horse.

***

When the Confederates reached the crest of Cemetery Ridge they found the Union infantry fresh and waiting for them. But they were not alone. One cannon remained at the top of the hill, and Gordon was holding the lanyard. He watched the rebels coming up the slope. Without difficulty or hesitation, he pulled the rope. The resounding blast signaled the charge of Colonel Devereux's men.

The resulting onslaught was swift and complete. Gordon watched as the 19th Massachusetts and the 42nd New York crashed into the Confederate mob inside the angle. The collision had an impact that caused a slight rebound effect. They struggled and they fought. Men picked up rocks and threw them at each other.

***

The smoke was so thick and the noise so loud that confusion gripped the battlefield. Ray got separated from Mike. If a man fell wounded, he was immediately trampled to death. The ground ran red with blood.

The air would clear just long enough so that the men on both sides could see the other's madness.

Ray was knocked off his feet. He got hit in the left leg. A minie' ball had torn through the flesh and shattered his femur bone. He looked and saw his leg dangling backwards. "*Mike!*" He screamed.

Mike turned and saw Ray rolling on the ground. He immediately saw the condition of his leg and was aghast.

"Ray!" Mike yelled and ran to his side. He dropped to his knees and put Ray's leg into position. "What did you do... my God," Mike cried, blaming Ray for his injury.

Mike made a bandage from his shirt and carefully wrapped it around Ray's leg. He was tying off a tourniquet when he felt a blunt strike to the head. Mike keeled over, stunned. He hit the ground and struggled to stay awake, but fell unconscious.

The tide had turned. The Confederates were driven back. The rebels were now shattered and broken. Confederate battle flags fell, and the fighting was coming to an end.

One by one, then by twos, and then by threes, then finally by the hundreds, the men in gray and butternut began wandering back down the slope of Cemetery Ridge. They were on the retreat.

***

Gordon watched the slaughter from the top of the hill next to the cannon. He had no idea that Mike and Ray was part of the carnage, and at that moment he didn't care.

"Good work," said a Union officer standing nearby.

"Huh?" was all Gordon could manage to say in his state.

Lieutenant Milne grabbed Gordon by the coat and shook him, trying to pull his mind away from the fighting. "You did say that you are a doctor?"

Well... I did, didn't I," Gordon said as he recognized who was standing next to him.

Gordon and Milne watched some Union men helping the remaining Confederates over the stone wall: to complete their journey, only to be taken prisoner.

"Come on," Milne pulled on Gordon's coat. "They have a job for you."

***

The next thing Mike knew, he was on a stretcher being carried to the rear. The battle was over, but the painful memory was still vivid in his mind.

He looked for Ray and saw the field and the carnage. He heard men begging for water, horses writhing in their death agonies. The sickening stench of battle filled the air. Streams of blood gathered on the ground and ran along it from pool to pool. He saw smoke boil up from the battlefield. The image burned into his memory: the true picture of butchery and death that he would never forget. *But*, he wondered, *where was Ray?* Mike didn't see or hear him and had no idea if he was alive or dead.

Chapter Twenty-Eight

July 3, 1863
Eleventh Corps Field Hospital - 6:05 P.M.

Mike was taken to a field hospital that was set up in a two story stone farm house and summer kitchen.

The wounded were met by nurses who were doing an early form of triage. The most critical went inside first. The less critical waited outside.

Mike's head had been wrapped with a bandage by a steward earlier. The nurse lifted the dressing. "You'll need stitching. Put him over there with the others."

The attendants manhandled him and placed him on the ground outside the kitchen door. He leaned over to listen, trying to hear if Ray was inside, but all he could hear were shrieks and moaning. Mike scooted into the doorway to get a better look.

A busy nurse saw him. "Stop that, you'll get your turn," she yelled.

Mike pretended to faint. The nurse walked up to him and bent down to check. Mike acted like he was having a seizure. A doctor looked outside the door. "Nurse, get him in here."

"Steward, I need you," she yelled.

She and the steward carried Mike inside and sat him in a chair in the crowded, dimly lit kitchen. Mike straightened and acted like he had recovered.

The doctor examined his wound, "You can wait," he said and walked away.

"Feeling better, I see," the nurse said.

"I'm trying to find my friend," Mike whispered to her looking for compassion.

"I don't have time for this," she said, stood up, and walked outside.

"Love you, too," Mike said and began to look around the room trying desperately to find Ray. As his eyes adjusted to the low light, he smelled the stench of body odor and blood. He didn't see Ray, but he did get an eyeful of every wound known to man. He saw suffering only war is capable of creating: men with arms, legs, or both, blown completely off. Those with gut wounds were made comfortable while they waited to die.

In the center of the room was the operating table. The surgeons, with their sleeves rolled up, worked by candlelight and the available light from open windows.

The men were placed upon the pine table only to have their limbs hacked off by the surgeon's saw.

The surgeons operated with their sleeves rolled up and their linen aprons were smeared with blood. Men screamed in pain, straining their lungs. "Please, leave me alone. Don't cut me please, please. I'll be good, I promise." The men begged and pleaded.

During the operations, the disgusting odor of fecal matter and urine circulated when the young men expelled their bodily functions. Some vomited before they were even touched. The thought of the torture alone was enough.

Mike gagged and fought the sensation of becoming sick himself.

"We're almost out of ether, doctor," a nurse said.

"Morphine then," the young surgeon yelled.

"Out of that, too," she said.

"Give 'em, laudanum," another surgeon said.

"That'll have to do," said the young surgeon.

One surgeon placed his knife between his teeth and quickly wiped the blood and puss from the previous patient off the table with a towel. He wiped his brow and said, "Next," and the next patient was placed upon the table.

He examined the wound, took in a breath, and let it out slowly. He took the knife from between his teeth, wiped it once on each side across his blood-stained apron, and began to cut.

"Leave me alone, I'm okay, don't do that, don't do that," the man screamed.

After their amputations were completed, they were placed on the floor. They begged, "Please, just let me die."

The pans on the floor filled with limbs. And when they overflowed, the limbs would hit the floor with a resounding *thud*. Pools of blood soaked into the planks of the wooden floor.

Never was a word so feared among the men, than the dreaded word, "next," when spoken by the surgeons.

Mike heard a commotion over by the window. A patient was complaining to one of the doctors. He wanted to be treated right then and now.

He leaned toward the racket and squinted both eyes to get a better look of who it was. To his surprise, it was Ray. *Should have known*, Mike thought.

"Union men first, and that is final," the doctor said and walked away.

Mike got up and walked over to Ray. "You okay?"

"Mike! Help me, Mike, I'm bleeding to death and nobody cares around here."

"Here, let me have a look." Mike began to examine his leg; it was a compound fracture. "Damn, Ray, it's broke. The bullet ripped right through."

"Can you fix it?"

"I'll need to clean it before I can splint and dress it."

"I'm dying here, Mike."

"Okay, okay, let me see if someone will help."

As Mike looked around, a young doctor turned and saw him. Mike was waving his arms for him to come. The young doctor walked toward him.

Mike was speechless. It took a moment, but then he was sure. "Gordy?"

Gordon stared—his mind seemed to be processing—then he realized it, too. "Mike, is that really you?"

Mike grabbed his hand and shook it, then pulled him into his chest and gave him a big man hug. "Jesus, Gordy, sure glad to see you." Then Mike remembered why he was looking around in the first place. "Ray needs help."

"Let me have a look," Gordon said and began to examine Ray's leg.

"I'm afraid that leg needs to come off to save your life," Gordon said.

"What! Why? It's only broke!"

"In this day and age, that's the treatment. Gangrene will set in, and you'll die."

"Then I'll die," Ray said.

"What if we get him back to our world?" Mike asked of Gordon.

"You mean back to our own time?" Gordon asked.

"Yes."

"How?" Gordon asked.

"We need to get to the barn where the box is," Mike said.

"What box? What barn?"

"The tinderbox."

"Tinderbox?" Gordon was puzzled for a moment. "Oh, the box with the poem."

"Yes, that's what got us here. And we need to get to the barn. I was hoping before Jake and Earl."

"Who the hell are Jake and Earl?" Gordon said getting even more confused.

"It's a long story, I'll tell you about it when we get out of here."

"Yeah, how you plan to do that?" Gordon asked.

"What the hell do you think you're doing?" Sergeant Smith interrupted.

Gordon recognized him right away and began to tremble. Mike had seen Gordon scared before, but never like this.

"What part of Union men first, don't you understand?" Smith said.

"Sorry, Mike, can't help now, gotta go," Gordon said and scurried off.

Even though Smith was a huge man, Mike didn't care. "Hey, someone's got to help my friend here," Mike said.

Sergeant Smith glared at Mike with his hollow black eyes. Mike felt fear rise within him. He felt as if he was looking into the eyes of the devil. Mike suppressed his fear and glared back.

Smith, not getting the reaction he hoped for, turned and walked away.

Mike turned to Ray. "I'll fix it," Mike said and walked to a table where some bandages were. He picked up several and grabbed a box. He broke the box's sides off to use as splints. Then, he picked up a whiskey bottle, walked back to Ray, and started to work.

"I've got to clean the wound first. Grit your teeth, this is going to hurt."

"Okay, Mike."

Mike poured the whiskey on Ray's open flesh. Blood and whiskey poured onto the wooden floor. Ray gritted his teeth but let out a yell. "Give me that bottle."

Mike helped Ray drink what was left.

"I must align the broken bones, Ray."

"More whiskey," Ray begged.

"There is no more," Mike said as he grabbed Ray's leg. "Here we go, you ready?"

"Wait!" Ray said too late. Mike pulled the leg until the broken ends of the white bones grounded past one another and went back into the flesh and aligned.

Ray let out a scream that could have been heard in Baltimore, but in this little hospital unit, it was just one more and no one paid attention.

Since there was no way to stitch his leg, Mike wrapped it tight in gauze. Then he placed the wooden box's side boards on both sides of his leg and wrapped them in place with what was left of the gauze.

Ray was exhausted and near unconsciousness from the ordeal. Mike wiped the sweat from his own forehead and closed his eyes.

Gordon slipped away and walked back to Mike, keeping an eye on Smith, hoping his paperwork would keep him busy. "Mike, how's Ray doing?"

Mike opened his eyes, "We need to get out of here tonight if we're to save him."

"What were you saying about the tinderbox and the poem?" Gordon asked.

"If he looks up, get away, quick," Mike warned.

"I got that, alright," Gordon said.

"When you read the poem, from the tinderbox, it sent us back in time. We need to get to the barn and read it again to get us home. Tonight, when they're all sleeping and things quiet down, we'll just walk out of here."

"What do we do about Ray?" Gordon said.

"What did I tell you about conversing with the enemy?" Sergeant Smith yelled from his desk.

Gordon turned his back to the sergeant and handed Mike a couple of pills. Mike saw the bruises on Gordon's face.

"Give this to Ray. He'll need it for the pain." He quickly turned and walked away.

"How you get those bruises?" Mike tried to ask but it was too late; Gordon had left the area.

"So, do you think you're special?" a voice came from behind him. Mike quickly turned around. Sergeant Smith was standing directly in front of him.

"What's it to you, ass—" before Mike could finish Smith had spun him around and had a knife to his throat. "You mean nothing to me, but I'm about to teach ya that I'm everything to you. I have your life in my hands."

Mike struggled to get free, but Smith pressed the knife harder against his neck.

Gordon saw what was happening. "Stop!" He yelled from across the room. He ran to Mike's aid.

"And what are you going to do?" Smith asked and pointed the knife at Gordon. "I can kill him and you, and be justified in doing it."

A surgeon showed up. "You'll stop it now, that's an order sergeant."

Smith relaxed, and then pushed Mike away. "Just teaching these boys a lesson."

"I think they had more then their share of lessons today," the surgeon said.

Smith turned to Mike. "This is a long way from being over." He walked back to his desk.

Mike and Gordon stared at each other.

The surgeon turned to them. "We'll be done with the Union men shortly. Then we'll amputate his leg."

Mike looked at Gordon. "We can't let that happen."

"Sir, may I interject a thought?" Gordon said.

"What is it?" The surgeon asked.

"We're out of ether and it's getting late and we all had a very long day, can we wait until morning when supplies get here?"

"You have a point, but we'll have to get started first thing in the morning."

"Thank you, sir," Gordon said. Then he turned to Mike. "We leave tonight, right after I take care of that bastard sergeant."

Chapter Twenty-Nine

July 3, 1863
Eleventh Corps Field Hospital - 8:31 P.M.

Now that most of the major wounds and amputations were carried out and bandaged, Gordon had leave to help Ray without Smith getting on his case about it.

Mike was rubbing Ray's head when Gordon walked over. "Mike, I want to suture Ray's leg, they'll let me now."

"Sure," Mike said.

"Then after that I want to look at your head wound."

"Worry about him," Mike said.

Gordon knelt next to Ray and examined his wound. Ray opened his eyes, and felt tremendous pain in his left leg. "Make it stop!"

Gordon had unwrapped his bandages. "Steward, bring me what's left of the ether and thread for sutures."

Mike knelt down beside Gordon. "How's it look?"

"Pus, we need to keep it clean so that gangrene doesn't set in before we have a chance to get him to a real hospital."

A surgeon walked over and knelt down beside Gordon. He examined the wound, too. "Laudable pus, it's a good sign, son, you do good work," the surgeon said and walked to the next patient.

"That's why we need to leave," Gordon said to Mike.

"Do you have any alcohol here?" Mike asked.

"Only whiskey... it's mostly alcohol."

"Okay," Mike said and stood up and walked to the table where there were a few whiskey bottles left. He picked up one and walked back.

The young steward came back. "Sir, we're all out of cat-gut and ether."

"Shit." Gordon thought for a moment and then snapped his fingers. "I need you to do me another favor."

"Yes, sir?"

Go outside and cut the lower half of a horse's tail off and bring it to me."

"Cut off the tail of a horse?"

"Lower half, soldier."

"Sir, yes, sir." The steward picked up the shears and left the room, shaking his head.

Gordon started a pot of water on the wood stove. He walked to one of the guards. "Let me have your bayonet."

"My bayon... why?" The guard asked confused.

"Just hand it over, please."

The guard unsheathed his bayonet and handed it to Gordon.

"What are you doing?" Mike asked.

"Watch and learn, my friend."

The steward got back with the tail. "Sir, what do you want me to do with it, sir?"

"Place it in the pot."

"Into the boiling hot water, sir?" The young man was dumbfounded.

"That's what I said."

"Yes, sir." The steward carefully placed the tail into the boiling water.

Gordon began to stir the hair with the bayonet like it was spaghetti. "Need to clean this up, if I'm to use it for stitches."

"You're kidding me right?" Mike said.

"Easy Mike, it'll be cleaner than what they previously used."

"Why?"

"Because, boiling kills the germs that they don't know anything about yet," Gordon explained in a low voice.

"I knew that," Mike said defensively.

Using the bayonet, Gordon took out a clump of horse hair and placed it on the table to straighten. Then, with needle and his makeshift thread, he walked back to Ray. "Here we go, Ray, let's see how this works."

When Gordon poured the whiskey on Ray's wound, he recoiled in pain and let out a scream that scared the shit out of Gordon, who jerked back himself.

"Easy, Ray," Gordon said. He composed himself and laid Ray back down.

Gordon began to sew using the horse hair. Mike watched every movement as if he was evaluating Gordon's skills.

"Don't you have any Lidocaine?" Ray managed to choke out.

"Sorry, we're all out of Lidocaine, today," Gordon said in a low voice. "Hold still."

Gordon finished the last stitch in Ray's leg and bandaged it. He turned to Mike. "We need to get him to a real hospital or we will have to amputate that leg."

"We'll leave ASAP," Mike said.

"Let me have a look at that, Mike."

"I'm okay."

"Let me see for myself."

Mike sat in a chair and Gordon pulled down his bandage. "Jesus, Mike, you have a three-inch gash in the back of your head. You're going to need stitches."

Mike was looking at Gordon's face and hands and saw the wounds and bruises. "What happen to you?"

"Don't change the subject."

"No really, what the hell happened?" Mike said.

"That sergeant over there, Smith, before this job he was deep into torture. He beat me until I told him whatever he wanted to hear."

"That son-of-a-"

"Let me take care of him in my own way, okay, Mike." Gordon interrupted.

"Okay, but if you need help—"

"I know who to call. Now let me help you."

Mike looked over at Ray. He was already unconscious.

"Here, drink this," Gordon shoved the bottle of whiskey in Mike's face.

Mike took a long pull of it. "I'm ready," he said and gritted his teeth.

Gordon poured some of the whiskey into a soft cloth and dabbed the back of Mike's head with it. Mike jumped in pain. "Watch that."

"Easy, Mike," Gordon said.

He began to sew up the three-inch gash. Mike could feel each and every stitch burning into his flesh. "That hurts like a bitch, I'll have you know." Mike gritted his teeth harder and endured the pain. When Gordon was done, he bandaged Mike's head. "There you go, good as new," Gordon sounded pleased with his work.

Some of the moaning had quieted down. The amputated arms and legs had been gathered for burial. The stewards had begun the tedious job of getting the blood up from the wooden floor. The blood smeared and got into the cracks between the boards.

Mike saw the nurses dressed in white gowns with their hair pulled back into buns. They knelt down beside the men and changed their bandages and checked their wounds.

The volunteers arrived wearing white aprons over any dress they had, which was mostly black. After the older, stern nurses gave the young women volunteers direction, they busied themselves comforting the young men, too.

As the minutes ticked by, every now and then, between the cries and moans, the low, lonely voice of some young soldier was heard Saying, "I want my mother."

Mike was trying to steal away the hours and sleep when he felt the soft caress of a hand over his forehead. The touch was cool. It was followed by the sweet smell of lavender.

Mike's eyes opened and a smile came across his face. "Sarah... what are you doing here?"

"I am a volunteer today," she said, "I'm here to see that you get well."

"Who might this lovely lady be?" Gordon asked, standing right behind her.

"You remember. She's the woman in white I've been chasing," Mike said. He saw the quizzical look on Gordon's face. "The one from the road."

"The one you almost ran over?" Gordon remembered.

"The same; her name is Sarah."

"How did she get here? Does she have something to do with the mess we're in?" Gordon asked.

"Calm down, she's trying to help us," Mike said.

"Well then maybe she can help us the hell out of here."

From her apron she produced a special salve that she concocted at home from her herb garden.

"What is that?" Gordon demanded.

"This will accelerate the healing process."

"Sounds like witchcraft to me," Gordon said.

"Keep your voice down. If you want to get out of here, and I assume you do, Ray needs to heal. He can't manage the terrain in pain."

"What do you think you're doing?" Sergeant Smith was once again standing right behind them.

Mike jumped. "Good evening sergeant," Sarah said.

"There's no fraternizing with the enemy," he said coldly.

"I'm not. I'm here to take care of our patients."

"I don't want to see you hanging around this scum of the earth. Do you hear me?"

"Trouble here, Sarah, dear?" A charge nurse asked.

"Just that this sergeant doesn't want me to do my job."

"Is that right, sergeant?"

"I want her to take care of our own, not this rebel scum."

"They're now all our wounded and we'll take care of all of them. Carry on, Sarah."

"I'm the boss here," Sergeant Smith said.

"You may be in charge of the building, but I'm in charge of the wounded. Now, back to your duties. I assume, sergeant, you do have duties of your own?" she turned and walked away.

"Find someone else to help," Sergeant Smith said to Sarah as he walked back to his desk.

Sarah, ignoring Smith, knelt down beside Mike and lifted his dressing. She examined the wound. "Nice stitching," she mentioned.

"Thanks," Gordon said.

Then she brought out a jar from under her apron. She opened it and applied the herbal salve to the wound under his dressings. She was extra gentle so as not to hurt him. "What is it exactly?" Gordon asked somewhat concerned.

"A blend of herbs that, I assure you, is perfectly safe."

"I trust you," Mike said. "Go ahead."

"Get your rest," she whispered in Mike's ear.

She got up and walked to Ray. She saw Ray's leg. "Lord, what have they done?" She lifted his leg, but couldn't hold it when she attempted to unwrap the bandages.

"Here, let me help you," Gordon said, as he knelt down beside her. He held Ray's leg up for her.

"I won't take apart the dressing. I'll just rub the ointment on the outside. It'll soak through and do some good."

"Hope you're right," Gordon said.

She opened it and the smell was pungent. She massaged it into the gauze making sure it soaked through. "There, that should do it."

Ray was trying to respond but couldn't.

Sarah stood up and saw the sergeant staring at her. She wanted to walk back to Mike when Gordon stopped her. "Can you put some of that on my... grand...friend over there?"

"Sure," Sarah said with her soft reassuring voice.

Gordon noticed how radiant she was.

She walked to Mortimer and knelt down beside him.

"Are you an angel?" Mortimer asked.

"No, but I am here to help you," Sarah said.

"You're not here to take me to Heaven?"

"Good Lord, no," She said and turned him on his side. "I'm here to make you feel better."

She removed his bandage and rubbed what was left of the salve on his wound, then replaced the dressing. "You'll be just fine."

She stood up and looked into Gordon's eyes. "Your grandfather is doing just fine."

Surprised, Gordon had to ask. "How did you know he was my grandfather?"

She leaned in close so no one else could hear. "You're right, I'm a witch," she straightened and gave Gordon a wink.

Gordon stood there for a long moment with his mouth open, and then managed to say, "Thank you."

She walked over to Mike. "Rest now, I'll be back with some soup."

"Sarah, we must leave tonight," Mike said sadly.

"I know, and I will help you."

Mike placed his hand on her arm. He felt the contours of her skin as he moved down to her hand. She smiled and took his hand and gently squeezed. Mike relaxed. He felt better already.

"I've got to go, but I'll be back. You can count on it," she told Mike.

She stood up and started for the door. She gave them a little wave and walked out.

Mike lay on his back staring at the ceiling smiling from cheek to cheek. The girl of his dreams had just entered his life. The sad part was that he had to leave her.

But someone else had entered his life also. It was the huge Sergeant Smith, and he was standing right in front of them again. He had gotten up from his chair and walked over without Mike seeing. "You boys comfortable are ya?"

"Yes, why, thanks for asking," Mike said sarcastically.

"Check that attitude of yours, you sum-bitchin' trader. I better not catch any ya'll fraternizing with our womenfolk. You got that?"

"Mike, let me informally introduce you to Sergeant Earnest Smith," Gordon said.

"Ain't done with you neither. Who'd you think you are? You might have them fooled, but I knows you're nothing but a sniveling little coward."

"Watch who you're calling a coward," Mike said.

"What you gonna do, boy?"

Sergeant Smith walked directly to Mike. He was about to strike when Mike came up and knocked him flat on his ass. He started to get up when Mike kicked him in the teeth. "Bigger they are, harder they fall."

Guards and doctors came running. They all met where Mike was standing over the sergeant.

"Lock him up!" Smith yelled from the floor, mad as a hornet.

"Having trouble with the prisoners, sergeant?" The surgeon asked.

Smith realized he didn't have a good explanation for harassing patients, even if they were prisoners.

"No trouble," he said as he got up off the floor holding his mouth and spitting blood.

"You want me to look at that for you?" the surgeon asked the sergeant.

"I'll be alright. Guards, back to your posts."

The surgeon walked away and the guards walked to their posts. One guard took his bayonet from the table and slipped it back into its scabbard.

Smith turned to Mike and Gordon. "Both you, listen up. Mark my words, you two won't make it to Fort McHenry."

Chapter Thirty

July 3, 1863
Eleventh Corps Field Hospital - 10:01 P.M.
When Sarah got back, she brought her special chicken broth in a large pot and loaves of freshly-baked bread. The room was crowded with the wounded soldiers. Most were quiet, exhausted from their wounds.

She picked up several small bowls and walked directly to Ray and sat down beside him. "Are you awake?"

Ray opened his eyes. "Sarah?"

"Don't talk, just drink this." She ladled out some soup in a bowl and hand fed him.

Mike felt strangely jealous watching her care for Ray.

"I've added a healing herb, it should make you feel better and dull your pain," she said. Ray finished his soup, and Sarah stood. "Get some rest," she added, and then walked to Mike. "Would you like some soup?"

"Yes," Mike said with glee in his eyes, now that her attention was on him. She dipped a bowl and handed it to him. Mike began to eat. She ladled out one more and handed it to Gordon.

"This is really good," Mike said.

"Your culinary skills are exceptional," Gordon added.

She broke off a piece of the homemade baked bread and handed it to Mike and another piece to Gordon. Mike leaned over to Gordon. Sarah leaned in also to hear what Mike had to say. In a hushed but stern voice he outlined his plan. "Ray's not going to make it if we don't get out of here. And I mean now. Sarah, I need you to distract the sergeant over there, while we sneak out the back door and bee-line it back to the barn," Mike said.

The Final Charge

"What about Ray?" Gordon asked.

"We carry him. See that stretcher against the wall? Get it and bring it here while Sarah talks to the sergeant."

"What do you want me to say?" She asked.

"I'll leave that up to you," Mike said.

Suddenly, Sergeant Smith was behind her. He pulled her up by her hair and pushed her until she hit against the wall. Mike became infuriated and stood up.

"I said no fraternizing with the enemy. I warned you once," Smith said.

Then he turned to see Mike right behind him. "I'll blow your God damn head off your shoulders if I catch you talking to her again," he warned.

Sarah snatched up a surgeon's knife from a small table and pointed it at Sergeant Smith.

"You're not going to touch them," she said angrily.

She poked at his chest. "One more profanity, one more threat, from that indecent tongue of yours and I'll hush you forever."

Smith looked at her with the dark, empty eyes of a psychopath. He moved toward her and, before she plunged the knife into his chest, Mike caught her arm. "Not now," Mike gave her a look. His touch calmed her immediately.

"If you say so, Michael."

She lowered the knife and placed it back on the table. Smith pushed her against the wall once more. "Why spoil the fun, we were just getting started," Smith said, holding her there.

The charge nurse walked over to find out what was all the commotion about. "Trouble here, Sarah?" The nurse asked.

"No trouble here, right, Sarah?" Sergeant Smith said and let go of her.

Sarah hesitated for a moment. "That's right."

Smith saw Gordon holding his bowl of soup and took it from him. "Thanks for the soup," he said with a smirk and contempt for Gordon. He began to walk away, but turned back toward Sarah and stared at her with cold black eyes. "You don't want to test me."

A shiver went down her spine. He turned and walked back to his desk with the soup. The charge nurse was right behind him. "Who do you think you are?"

"I'm the one in charge of this place," Sergeant Smith said, and sat back down at his desk. He began to eat Gordon's soup. The charge nurse was beside herself and walked away.

Sarah turned to Gordon. "I'll fix you another."

"That's okay, Sarah. Give what you have to the wounded." Gordon said.

A major walked over to Sergeant Smith. "Be ready to move out on a moment's notice."

Mike overheard him. Sarah turned to Mike. "Take this." She slipped him a hand written map of the area. Mike was surprised, but pleased.

"With this map you can find your way back to the barn."

"I don't know what to say." Mike said.

"I don't want you to go, but I also know you must help your friends."

"I don't want to go either," Mike said.

"We all have our paths to follow," she told him.

"Are you good with the plan, Gordy?" Mike asked.

"Carrying Ray to the barn, sure I'm good, but I hope Ray can take the strain."

"Be sure to review the map before you leave. It's awful dark outside," Sarah instructed.

Mike nodded in agreement and looked at Gordon for confirmation. Gordon nodded. He was good with the plan.

"Well, here we go." Sarah walked over to Sergeant Smith's desk. The sergeant was feeling sick and looked up from his paperwork to see her standing there.

Meanwhile, Gordon walked to the stretcher and stopped. He noticed a rack of steward frock coats hanging and grabbed the largest. He saw that a couple of straps used to tie down the patents were hanging on the wall. He took them and the stretcher and headed back to Mike.

Sarah stood in front of the sergeant for a long moment, seemingly to build her courage. "I would like to apologize for my action. You're right. I shouldn't fraternize with the enemy."

"Well, I'm glad you've come to your senses," Smith said.

Her lips began to quiver. "You are a man's man, aren't you, Sergeant?"

"Well, if you mean fightin' well, that means killin' and that's what I'm trained to do. But if you mean lovin' I'm self trained for that."

She looked at him and got sick at the thought, but she had set her trap and he stepped right in it.

He stood holding his stomach and lustily looked her square in the eyes. "How 'bout me and you taking a little break from all of this. I'll make it worth your while," he said and licked his lips. Sarah, not only disgusted by the remark, but now frightened, swallowed hard building up her courage.

Suddenly, she slapped him. He took the full force of her slap, and leaned back away from her reach. Sick, he sat back down in his chair.

Two guards saw what happened and came to his defense.

At the same time, the charge nurse came to Sarah's defense.

Gordon gave Mike the coat and whispered, "Here, this will be your disguise."

Mike quickly put the steward's frock coat on. It was a bit small, but he managed. They both turned to Ray. Mike grabbed his legs and Gordon took his arms and they placed him on the stretcher. Ray yelped, but kept his cool; he was now completely awake and alert.

Meanwhile, the charge nurse was livid. "What is going on in here?"

"She started it," Sergeant Smith said. Then he belched.

"Explain yourself, Sarah," the charge nurse said.

"He insulted me."

"How?"

Sarah leaned toward the nurse. "He asked for...um, favors."

"Oh my Lord! What kind of animal are you?" The charge nurse said.

"You're mad, both of ya. I'm over here minding my own business. She came up to me." Just then Smith, while holding his belly, had a thought of the deception. Smith tried to look around her, but Sarah kept blocking his view.

Finally, Smith had had enough and pushed her aside. In the distance he saw two empty blankets on the floor. The prisoners were gone. He looked around and saw that Gordon was gone, too. His face twisted in anger and became several shades of green. He looked like the devil had just possessed him.

"They've escaped! After them, men! And don't forget that so-called doctor is with them." Smith threw up on the floor.

The guards ran to the racks to get their gear, turned and ran for the rear door.

"Don't let them get away," Smith said spitting again. "Shoot them on sight, that's an order!" He yelled as he spit out the last of his vomit. He stumbled to the rack, holding his belly, and grabbed his equipment. He bent over in pain, and then started for the door, moving slowly across the room.

He got to the rear door, and while holding onto the jamb, he turned to Sarah. "I'll deal with you later," he said, then continued out the door to the squad of men waiting for orders.

Chapter Thirty-One

July 3, 1863
Outside the Hospital - 11:17 P.M.

Holding one end of the stretcher, Mike waited a moment for his eyes to adjust to the darkness. With Gordon on the other end, they carried Ray along a footpath that Sarah had showed them on the map.

They walked right by two soldiers having a conversation. Mike kept straight and did not say a word.

"You there, steward, where you going?" a soldier asked.

"Too crowded here, told to take 'em down the way," Mike said and kept walking.

"Need any help?" soldier asked.

"Nah, we got it," Mike said and picked up the pace.

Once they got out of sight of the soldiers, Mike felt a little more at ease.

Ray's weight shifted on the stretcher. "Got to set him down, Mike," Gordon said.

"Damn, Ray, you need to lose some weight," Mike said putting the stretcher down.

Storm clouds had rolled in and it began to drizzle.

"Okay, let's use these straps to secure him to the stretcher," Gordon said.

"Good idea," Mike answered.

"With this rain we don't need him to slide off," Gordon said.

They picked up the stretcher and followed a foot path.

"Can it get any darker? It's hard to see the path," Mike complained.

Finally, they came to a dirt lane.

"Need to put him down," Gordon said out of breath.

Mike placed the stretcher on the ground.

"I've got blisters on both palms," Gordon said.

"Let me tie a strap, I'll drag him," Mike suggested.

"I'm sorry, Mike," Gordon said.

"Don't worry about it, I can do this," Mike said.

Mike wrapped his hands around the strap and picked up the stretcher and dragged Ray until they came to a wide road he believed to be Taneytown Road. Ray was starting to moan.

"Hold up, Mike, let me check Ray."

Mike needed to rest anyway. He placed the stretcher down.

Gordon began to examine Ray. "He's going into shock. We really need to get him to a hospital."

"What do you think we're doing, for Christ sakes?"

"Okay, okay, I know that," Gordon said, "Just that he really needs an IV to replenish his fluids.

"We're doing the best we can," Mike said.

"I know, Mike. It's just that the rain is making things worse."

Mike took this moment of rest for an opportunity to ask something that had been bothering him since they left the field hospital. "What happened to Smith?"

"What about him?" Gordon asked. A funny look came across his face.

"He got sick awfully fast," Mike said.

"I knew he couldn't resist taking my soup, especially if I held it in front of him, so I laced it," Gordon said with a chuckle.

"Laced it with what?

"Strychnine."

"Damn. Remind me not to piss you off. Was it enough to kill him?" Mike asked.

"No, just enough to make him damn sick. He'll wish he was dead."

This time Mike gave a chuckle. He took the map from his coat pocket and started to look at it. The rain was falling harder now and getting the map wet. The pencil drawing started to blur. Mike looked up from the map. "You ready?"

"I'm following you," Gordon said.

Mike picked up the stretcher and started up the road, dragging Ray. He followed Taneytown Road towards town, the only lights visible. Suddenly, Mike saw a silhouette of a man crossing the road and he stopped. He carefully sat the stretcher down.

Gordon stood there with a surprised look on his face. Mike moved along the wet ground on his knees back to Gordon. "Sentries at the intersection."

"You sure? How the hell can you see in this darkness?" Gordon asked.

"He walked through the town's light," Mike said.

"We passed a path back there," Gordon mentioned.

"We did?"

"Just a few yards," Gordon said.

"Okay, do you think you can drag him for a while? I've got blisters now," Mike asked.

"Sure," Gordon tore his shirt in strips and wrapped his hands to protect them.

Gordon picked up the stretcher. He doubled back to the path, which was just a few yards away. Mike was trying to see the rain soaked map. It was just one big smudge now, but he made out a bridle path Sarah had penciled in. "Think it goes to the barn?" Mike said.

"Let's hope, and soon, he's heavy as hell," Gordon said.

Gordon, now dragging Ray, began to follow the narrow, winding pathway through the high grass with Mike right behind them. The rain danced in the grass making a steady, musical sound.

"How much farther?" Ray managed to weakly ask.

"How should I know?" Mike said frustrated.

"Hang in there, Ray," Gordon said.

Through the heavy downpour, Gordon lost the trail. "Can't see, Mike."

"To the right," Mike said.

Gordon dragged Ray as far as he could. He fell to his knees, "I can't go any farther."

"That's okay, you did good, I'm rested now."

Mike was renewed when he saw what he believed to be another road up ahead. He grabbed the straps tightly with his bare hands and started to pull. Without protection for his hands, his blisters opened. Ignoring the pain, he pulled the stretcher to the road and set Ray down.

Mike looked at his hands. They were bleeding. He pulled out Sarah's map again and looked at it. He crumpled it up and threw it. "Useless. I say we go left."

"Are you sure?" Gordon asked."

"As sure as I'm gonna get."

"Alright, like you always say, lead, follow, or get out of the way."

With his hands bleeding, Mike once again picked up Ray and dragged him up the washed out road, listening and looking for any signs of movement, civilian or soldier, not caring which. "See anything?"

"Nope," Gordon said.

Mike stayed to the right side of the road. He didn't want to get too turned around. With the downpour, the drainage ditch was filling with water. Then he saw a light, like a streetlamp, way up the road. Then he heard voices. "Stop!" Mike fell to his knees in pain.

"What is it?" Gordon asked.

"Soldiers. We need to stay out of sight."

"Think they're looking for us?" Gordon asked.

"Yeah, and since you poisoned Smith, he'll be out for revenge."

"Oh, crap, seemed like a good idea at the time."

"Where they're standing, I think is the barn," Mike said.

"Finally," Ray muttered.

"Don't worry, Ray, we'll get you home," Gordon said trying to comfort him.

"My hands are killing me. We'll both have to carry the stretcher again. We'll stay low and go around to the back. There's a side door. Got it?"

"Got it," Gordon whispered with a sigh of relief.

Mike stood up. The fist that hit him seemed to come from nowhere. Mike spun around holding his jaw and there was Jake standing in the rain. "Shoulda killed ya when I had the chance."

Jake held an Enfield rifle high in the air and swung it. It hit Mike on the right side of his chest.

Mike grabbed it with a grunt, trapping it under his right armpit. He rotated and took the rifle away from Jake then pointed it at him and pulled the trigger. A clap was heard as the hammer landed on the cap nipple. But there was no bang.

"Powder's wet," Jake said with a smile.

Mike looked at Jake and then saw Earl beating Gordon with his bare hands. Jake charged at Mike but, quickly, Mike executed a beautiful lower the stock-strike maneuver he had practiced during the bayonet exercise and struck Jake in the groin.

As Jake went to his knees in pain, holding his crotch, Mike swung the rifle and connected with Earl's right ribcage, knocking him down. Earl moaned in pain as he went to the ground.

"You okay, Gordy?" Mike shouted.

"Look out," Gordon yelled.

Jake was off the wet ground with a rock in his hand. When Mike spun around his jaw met Jake's rock. Mike went to the ground losing the rifle. Jake quickly picked it up and stood over Mike.

"Time for nighty, night," Jake said, and then struck Mike with the stock of the rifle across his head. As the blood flew, Mike went unconscious.

"Mike!" Gordon bellowed while sitting on Earl seeing Mike get hit. Earl pushed him off and Gordon scrambled to his feet and ran towards Jake, shouting "Nooo, you son-of-a-bitch!"

He swung at Jake, but the punch was blocked. Gordon swung again and Jake grabbed his fist.

Earl grabbed Gordon from behind and held him. Jake delivered another blow to Gordon's head with the rifle butt. Blood flew as Gordon gave out a yelp and went down.

Jake turned to Mike and dragged him to the edge of the road, while Earl rolled Gordon to the edge.

"What about the other one?"

"Take care of him first," Jake said.

They walked over to Ray, who was still tied to the stretcher.

"No, no, what you gonna to do? Leave me alone," Ray shouted and struggled to break free.

They picked up the stretcher with him screaming, and at the count of three, threw Ray and the stretcher into the ditch. Ray let out a painful yell and sank down into the water.

Jake pulled his knife from his boot and was about to cut Mike and Gordon's throats before tossing them into the ditch, when he heard a noise.

"What's that?"

"What's what?" Earl asked.

The rain was heavy, making it hard to hear.

"Someone's coming, quick kick 'em in the ditch" Jake said.

As Jake put his knife back in his boot, Earl kicked Gordon into the ditch. Jake kicked Mike into the ditch and then, quickly, they both hid along the road in the tall grass opposite the ditch. They stayed low and waited.

A squad of riders was coming fast up the road. They slowed down as they passed. They went by without noticing anything. After they were gone, Jake stood up. "Let's go."

Earl got up off the ground, holding his right side. "Ain't ya gonna kill 'em?" he asked.

"No need, the way the ditch is filling up with water. Looks like the rain will take care of that fer us."

Lighting flashed across the sky, followed by a large boom of thunder.

Jake began to run up the washed-out, muddy road with Earl following right behind.

Chapter Thirty-Two

July 3, 1863 - The Ditch - 11:45pm.

Mike broke the water gasping for air. He spit out what water he had swallowed and looked around. He saw Gordon floating face down, but no sign of Ray. He pulled Gordon's face from the water. Gordon took a breath, and began to struggle.

"It's me, Gordy. You're okay. Help me find Ray."

Gordon recovered and began to look around. He swished around desperately and felt something. "Here!"

Mike and Gordon grabbed the stretcher with Ray still tied to it and pushed it to the road surface.

Mike climbed out of the ditch and started to unfasten the straps. Gordon went to Ray's head and saw that he wasn't breathing and gave him a couple of breaths. Mike threw off the straps and Ray sat up, coughing water from his mouth. He took in a deep breath.

"You okay, Ray?" Mike asked.

"Think so," Ray managed to say. Then he felt the pain. "My leg, help me, Mike, my leg."

"We need to go." Mike worried that the army was still in pursuit of them. And he also knew that he had to stop Jake and Earl. In the distance, he could just make out the barn and farm house. He took off his steward frock coat. "We'll make a cradle out of my coat and carry him."

"Okay," Gordon agreed, not totally convinced it could be done.

Mike pushed the coat under Ray while Gordon sat him on it. Gordon grabbed one of the coat sleeves and pulled it behind Ray. Mike had the other. Gordon grabbed one of the tails of the coat and, along with Mike, brought the tails up between Ray's legs.

"Ready?" Mike asked.

"Ready," Gordon said.

They lifted Ray with a grunt and into the dark they started for the rear of the barn.

As they crossed the tall wet grass Gordon said, "I'm losing my grip." They only had a few more yards to go before Gordon lost his grip and Ray fell with a yelp.

"Sorry, Ray," Gordon said.

"I don't think I can take this much longer," Ray howled.

"Quiet, Ray. See anybody, Gordy?"

"Can't see anything."

"Can you continue?"

"I'll try," Gordon said.

Gordon adjusted his grip and they lifted Ray once more. This time they made it to the backyard of the farmhouse. Gordon had to put Ray down. "Need to rest."

"Okay, I'll carry him from here. You go around to the side door and see if it's clear."

"Got it. Give me Ray's lighter," Gordon said.

Mike took the lighter out of Ray's pocket and handed it to Gordon. He went off to sneak around to the side door.

***

Gordon slowly approached the door. He thought he heard a noise and looked around. He didn't know if it was on the inside, or if it had come from outside the barn. He placed his ear on the door to listen. Not hearing anything more, he placed his hand on the door handle.

***

Meanwhile, Mike waited for the all-clear. A few minutes went by and Mike saw a blue flash from inside the barn.

***

After stabbing Earl and leaving him to die in the hayloft, Jake, with the haversack of gold, quickly walked toward the barn's side door. He picked up the pace when he heard a noise. He didn't know if it was inside with him or coming from the outside. He paused at the door to listen.

"Who's here? He asked nervously as he looked around. At the exact moment that he took hold of the door handle, Gordon also grabbed it from the outside.

Jake, now in the 21st century opened the door and passed through Gordon who was still in the 19th century.

Once outside, Jake looked around. Not a sound was heard and no one seemed to be around. He walked to the road and stopped. He looked up at the stars in the early morning sky. Not a cloud could be seen. He looked down and wondered: *It was just raining, so why's the road so hard?* He stomped his foot on the hard macadam and walked into the middle of the road, looked up and saw two balls of fire coming right at him.

Suddenly, a car traveling at fifty miles per hour hit him. The black haversack with the gold went flying through the air. The car screeched to a halt, and the young nurse got out and ran back to him.

Jake laid in the street. The nurse saw what appeared to be a reenactor. She looked at her watch. It read five o'clock. "What in the world was he doing out here this early in the morning?" She then used her cell phone to call 911.

***

Gordon reappeared in the distance. He cupped his hand over Ray's lighter, lit it and waved it back and forth, then flipped it out. Mike, seeing this, picked up Ray with a grunt and threw him over his right shoulder. Ray cried out in pain.

"Come on, Ray, let's get to the barn."

When Mike got to the side door, Gordon had already opened it. Mike walked inside with Ray. No one was around. But there was a lantern lit on a wooden table.

"Anybody here?" Mike asked the darkness.

"I lit the lantern with Ray's lighter," Gordon said. "Put him on the table."

Mike carefully placed Ray on the table. Ray was out of it; he didn't even moan.

"You check Ray, I'll check the hayloft," Mike said.

"Sure, Mike." Gordon began to examine Ray's wound. The bandages were soaked and needed changing, but Gordon had nothing to use.

Mike grabbed a lantern from the rafter and lit it. He ran across the wooden floor to the hayloft, climbed the ladder, and looked around; nothing. Slowly he crawled to the corner holding the lantern over his head to see thinking he would see Earl, dead, in the corner.

He searched for the box but couldn't find it. Then he remembered; he looked into the hollowed out rafter: There it was. He took the tinderbox from its resting place and crawled back over to the ladder and climbed back down.

Back on the ground he walked over to Gordon and Ray.

"Do you have the box?" Gordon asked.

"Yes." Mike showed him the tinderbox.

"How's he doing?" Mike asked.

"We need to go. It may already be too late."

Ray didn't speak. His eyes were wide and distant. He looked up into nothingness, tears forming in the corners of his eyes. Shock had set in.

"Hold on, Ray," Mike said. We're gonna get you outta here." Before he could open the box, a musket ball tore through the barn wall, striking the table Ray lay on.

Mike covered his friend while Gordon crouched to the floor.

"We have you surrounded!" A familiar voice said. "Put down your arms and come out. You have one minute."

They heard the sound of heavy footfalls outside the barn. Mike crept to the wall and peered outside through a crack between the wooden boards.

"Be careful, Mike," Gordon said.

Mike saw the soldiers moving about like shadows. As he looked through the cracks between the boards, a single shot was fired almost tearing his head off. Mike stumbled back, checking his right ear to make sure it was still there.

"Are you alright, Mike?" Gordon asked while attending Ray.

"Soldiers are taking up positions surrounding the barn." Mike looked at Gordon and then Ray, who was lying helplessly on the table. He saw how desperate the situation had become. An overwhelming feeling of guilt washed over him. It had been his idea to come to the weekend reenactment. It had been his idea to check out the old red barn. It was he who forced Gordon to read the spell, sending them all back to this God-awful hell. And now, here they were trapped in this barn, surrounded by their soon-to-be executioners. "I'm sorry," Mike finally said.

Gordon looked at Mike and saw his sadness. "Sorry for what? We came together, we'll die together if need be, but we're not dead yet."

Mike straightened: the words Gordon spoke made him feel proud to be his friend.

Mike yelled through the cracks in the walls, "Okay, you win. We're not going to fight. Send someone in here to help our wounded friend and we'll come out together."

"What the hell are you doing?" asked Gordon.

"Buying time. I've got one chance to read this spell and get us home."

Suddenly, the side door burst open with a vicious crack. A huge silhouette of a man stood motionless in the doorframe. The ominous figure then moved into the light of a burning lantern. There stood Sergeant Earnest Smith with his grim reaper stare and his pistol drawn. He seemed bigger than any normal human being, twice the size of Mike.

He moved toward Gordon, who was still attending Ray.

"I won't let you hurt him, you son of a bastard!"

Smith smirked. "That's what I hoped you'd say." He raised his pistol, taking aim at Gordon's forehead. "You just made my -"

A violent strike from behind knocked the gun from Smith's hand. As Smith turned, Mike struck him again in the ribs with a two-by-four he found on the floor. Smith just stood there, taking the strikes as if nothing fazed him. Smith stripped the two-by-four from Mike's grip and dropped it on the floor. He punched Mike in the jaw, knocking him to the ground.

In an instant, a blade was drawn from Smith's belt. Mike became keenly aware of its presence and fought as hard as he could to avoid its glimmering death.

Smith delivered a crushing blow to Mike's throat with his elbow. Mike dazed and gasping for breath watched as Smith's knife rose into the air for the finishing blow, but Smith was struck once again. His knife fell from his grip as he went down.

Gordon stood over him holding the broken end of the shovel. When Smith tried to get to his feet, Gordon kicked him, and Smith grabbed his leg and threw him violently to the floor. Smith maneuvered and got on top of Gordon.

Still clenching his throat, Mike saw Smith go for the knife. Gordon held Smith back so that his fingers were just inches from getting the knife again when Smith put his hands around Gordon's throat.

Gordon felt the life draining from him when another strike knocked Smith to the floor. Mike stood there with the wooden bench from the table. Smith was stunned for a moment. Then, he reached for the knife a second time, but Gordon beat him to it. Smith tried to resist Gordon's attack, but it was too late. The blade of the knife pierced his throat and Gordon pushed it all the way down to the handle. "No more," Gordon said.

Smith's eyes glared wildly in disbelief at Gordon who was now only inches from his face. Gordon watched as Smith's eyes became distant and faded out with a sigh of his last breath.

Mike put his hand on Gordon's shoulder, breaking him from his madness. "We gotta hurry," he said, still rubbing his throat.

Suddenly, the wood of the barn around them began to crackle and splinter with musket fire from the Union men outside: They were acting on orders to open fire if Smith wasn't out with the prisoners in five minutes. A ball hit the lantern, knocking it down, and setting a hay bale ablaze. The flames shot up around them.

Mike and Gordon huddled around Ray. Mike opened the tinderbox and pulled out the hourglass. He turned the glass over and placed it on the table. The white sand started to pour. The heat and smoke became so thick and intense that Mike realized they all needed to get low.

Gordon instinctively knew what Mike wanted. They grabbed Ray and pulled him off the table. Ray hit the floor with a thud.

Mike reached up and grabbed the tinderbox. The hourglass was left on the table top. Mike quickly opened the tinderbox and brought out the parchment paper and unrolled it, revealing the mystical poem.

The barn had become a hellish inferno, glowing orange and red. The three men squeezed closer together, staying low to avoid gunshots and intense heat that was engulfing the barn.

Mike couldn't read the words with the barn being so hot and smoky. Then, he caught the scent of lavender and the space around them became cool. "Read the poem, Michael." It was Sarah protecting them. She held the flames back with her breath.

Mike began to read. *"Many paths through centuries fall - If change is what you seek."*

Mike choked from the smoke and gagged as he read. He coughed and Gordon yelled, "Read the poem!"

"Illumination shines true for all - Fulfillment for the meek."

As Mike finished the poem, the hourglass fell off the table and shattered into a thousand pieces. Then, part of the roof fell. A deafening roar crashed down around them, as if God Himself had slammed down his almighty gavel, delivering Judgment Day.

Then, there was silence.

Chapter Thirty-Three

Mike opened his eyes and the old barn was whole once again. There was light. Gordon was next to him, blood dripping down his face and all over his blue uniform. They exchanged looks of disbelief. Ray moaned.

Mike shook off his dreamlike state and leaned over Ray. "You okay?"

Ray just laid there, dazed, trying to talk, but before they could say anything, the two big barn doors pushed open and the light got brighter. There was a large shadow of a man standing directly in front of him. "Smith!" Mike lunged at him.

"Whoa there, pard, hold on." The man yelled, holding Mike back. "What's your problem?"

Mike's brown shirt was torn and spattered with blood. His forehead was wounded and he was filthy from the black powder.

"Only ten o'clock and it looks like you already been through a battle," the man said.

His voice was vaguely familiar to Mike.

"We just wanted to know if you guys are coming."

Mike looked hard, but the sunlight silhouetted the soldier so that he could not see his face.

"Who are you?" Mike finally asked.

"Tom, for Christ sakes."

"Tom? ... "Tom, who?" Mike asked.

"Pete the Pirate, Tom."

"As in Tree-Man? Mike asked.

"Whatever."

Mike relaxed. "I can't believe we're back." He swallowed hard and then slumped with relief. "We're back."

"What happened here?" Tom asked.

"We need to help Ray. Somebody call 911," Mike said.

"What the hell happened to him?" Tom asked.

"He broke his leg," Mike said.

Tom stood there in disbelief.

"Tom, call 911," Gordon said.

"Phone is back at camp."

"I've got mine," another reenactor said.

"How'd you get so cut up?" Tom asked.

"Long story," Mike said.

Mike and the others walked outside into the daylight and Mike covered his eyes until they adjusted to the bright sun.

"How'd you know we were in here?" Mike asked Tom.

"Saw your junker parked up the road from here. And then I heard noises coming from the barn."

The ambulance and the police finally showed up. The paramedics took one look at Ray immediately called for the helicopter.

After the flight paramedic checked his condition, Ray was given fluids and he regained consciousness. "Who did the work on his leg?" The flight paramedic asked.

"I did," Gordon said softly, not sure what the medic would say next.

"Good job, I'd say you saved his leg."

"Great," Gordon said with relief.

Mike helped the paramedics load Ray onto the chopper to be taken to shock trauma.

As the bird flew away, Gordon's thoughts turned to the tinderbox. "How did it work if the hourglass was broken?" Gordon asked, confused.

"The sand must have run completely through before it fell," Mike rationalized.

"The police are going to want to talk to you guys," Tom said.

Then Mike remembered. "Earl's body." He ran inside the barn to the hayloft. He knew the police would look eventually. Gordon ran after him. Mike climbed up and crawled over to where Earl should have been. But he was gone.

"Mike, is he there?" Gordon called out.

Mike, relieved, crawled back and climbed down the ladder. "Gone."

"How's that possible?"

"Don't ask me," Mike said and walked back outside.

Tom met them when they came out. "You guys look like shit. The ambo attendant wants to know if you're going to the hospital with them."

"What's today?" Mike asked.

"Saturday," Tom said.

"We were gone for only one night?" Mike said.

"So what do you want to do?" The paramedic asked.

"Drive ourselves," Mike finally said.

"Sign here," the medic said.

Mike signed, then Gordon signed, then the medic walked back to the ambulance.

"You two headed for the hospital?" A policeman asked.

"Yes," Mike said.

"We'll get your statements there." The officer walked to his cruiser.

Mike and Gordon began to walk back to Mike's truck. They both stopped and overheard Tom and the others talking as they headed back to the event grounds.

"Don't know what happened in there, but they look like they were dragged through hell." Tom said.

"Maybe they saw a ghost? You know Gettysburg is known as a hotbed for the paranormal," a reenactor with period wire-rim glasses commented as he flipped through his book.

Mike laughed and shook his head. "Come on."

As they walked around to the front of the barn, Mike stopped when they reached the road. "Jake left the barn with the gold, right?"

"Yeah."

"But, he didn't have the gold on him when the car hit him early yesterday morning."

"Right."

"So it must be around here someplace," Mike said.

"Guess so," Gordon said.

Mike pointed at a storm drain. "Did you notice that drain in front of the barn?"

"No, can't say I did," Gordon said.

"Let's have a look."

Mike walked over to the storm drain not ten feet from the front of the barn. It had a large gap from a missing grate that had broken. He watched as Tom and the other reenactors walked far out of sight. He knelt down to the grate and peered into the dark.

Gordon knelt down beside him. "Can't see anything."

Mike's eyes adjusted to the low light. "Wait, I see something. Help me move the grate."

"You sure you want to do that? What about the park rangers?"

"After what I've been through, they can't hurt me."

Gordon helped Mike pry up the grate and slide it to the side. Mike reached down for a black strap in the corrugated steel pipe and pulled out a haversack.

"Open it, Mike," Gordon said excitedly.

Mike undid the strap and opened the flap. He reached his hand in and pulled out a mint condition, twenty dollar double eagle gold piece.

"Holy sh... the lost Confederate gold," Gordon said.

Mike dumped the contents on the ground. Gordon counted thirty pieces.

"We're rich," Mike said.

"One problem," Gordon said.

"What's that?"

"Anything found on park property belongs to the park."

"Only you would worry about that."

"Maybe, if we turn it in, we'll get a reward."

"I got a better rule, finders keepers, losers weepers," Mike said.

While Mike studied one of the coins, he clasped his fingers into a fist and started to daydream. His thoughts went to Sarah, how good life could be with her. He truly missed her. "Love to go back, but how? The hourglass is broken. I'll never see her again."

"Hello, Mike," Sarah said standing behind him.

Mike rose and turned. "How is this possible?"

"Good to see you, too," Sarah said.

Mike smiled and embraced her. "It's really you."

"Sure it's me, expecting someone else?"

"Seriously, how's all this possible?" Mike asked.

"Yes, I would like to know that myself," Gordon said.

"The barn is a porthole. The tinderbox was a key. There are many keys to many portholes."

"What happened to Earl?" Mike asked.

"I got rid of Earl for us. He's still in the barn, only he's in 1863. Let them deal with him there."

"What about Jake?" Gordon asked.

"Let the police deal with him here as an anomaly."

"Wow, you're really something," Mike said.

Mike was overcome. He took her by the arm and brought her in close. Face to face, Mike couldn't resist. He leaned in and kissed her warmly on the mouth. She weakened and her body leaned against him. They embraced in earnest.

Gordon was putting the gold coins back into the black haversack. "Come on, get a room."

Sarah's face turned bright red. Gordon stood up and noticed something in the distance. He looked and froze in place.

"Let's go see how Ray's doing," Mike said.

Gordon didn't answer.

"What's wrong with you?"

Gordon stared beyond the barn.

"What are you looking at?" Mike turned to see.

"It's the Visitor Center," Gordon said.

"So... Oh my God, it can't be," Mike said.

They both stood there in total disbelief.

The Visitor Center's flags were flapping in the breeze. Mike was speechless. The flag they saw flying high over the Visitor Center was not old glory, but the Stars and Bars of the Confederate States of America.

Made in the USA
Charleston, SC
31 May 2011